Praise for Richard T. Ryan's S

Adventures

"The Vatican Cameos"

Winner of the Underground Book Reviews' "Novel of the Year" Award.

Winner Silver Medal in the Readers' Favorite book-award contest.

"[*The Vatican Cameos* is] an extravagantly imagined and beautifully written Holmes story." – Lee Child, NY Times Bestselling author and the creator of Jack Reacher

"Once you've read *The Vatican Cameos*, you'll find yourself eagerly awaiting the next in Ryan's series." – Fran Wood, What Fran's Reading for nj.com

"Richard T. Ryan's *The Vatican Cameos* is an excellent pastiche-length novel, very much in the spirit of the original Holmes stories by Sir Arthur Conan Doyle." – Dan Andriacco, author of a host of Holmes' tales as well as the blog, bakerstreetbest.com

"Loved it! A must read for all fans of Sherlock Holmes!" – Caroline Vincent, Bits about Books

"Richard Ryan channels Dan Brown as well as Conan Doyle in this successful novel." – Tom Turley, Sherlockian author

"If you enjoy deeply researched historical fiction, combined with not one but two mystery/thriller stories, then you will really enjoy this excellent Sherlock Holmes pastiche." – Craig Copland, author of New Sherlock Holmes Mysteries

"A great addition to the Holmes Canon. Definitely worth a read." – Rob Hart, author of *The Warehouse* and the Ash McKenna series

"*The Vatican Cameos* opens with a familiar feel for fans of Arthur Conan Doyle's original Sherlock Holmes stories. The plotting is clever, and the alternating stories well-told." – Crime Thriller Hound

"A masterful spin on the ageless Sherlock Holmes. Somewhere I'm certain Sir Arthur Conan Doyle himself is standing and cheering." – Jake Needham, author of the Jack Sheperd and Inspector Samuel Tay series

"The Stone of Destiny"

"Sometimes a book comes along that absolutely restores your faith in reading. Such is the "found manuscript of Dr. Watson, *The Stone of Destiny*. Exhilarating, superb narrative and a cast of characters that are as dark as they are vivid. ... A thriller of the very first rank." – Ken Bruen, author of *The Guards, The Magdalen Martyrs,* and many other novels, as well as the creator of the Jack Taylor series

"A wonderful read for both the casual Sherlock Holmes fan and the most die-hard devotees of the beloved character." – Terrence McCauley, author of *A Conspiracy of Ravens and A Murder of Crows*

"Somewhere Sir Arthur Conan Doyle is smiling. Ryan's *The Stone of Destiny* is a fine addition to the Canon." – Reed Farrel Coleman, NY Times Bestselling author of *What You Break*

"Full of interesting facts, the story satisfies and may even have you believing that Holmes and Watson actually existed." – Crime Thriller Hound

"Ryan's Holmes is the real deal in [*The Stone of Destiny*]. One hopes the author is hard at work on the next adventure in this wonderfully imagined and executed series." – Fran Wood, What Fran's Reading for nj.com

"Mystery lovers will enjoy reading *The Stone of Destiny: A Sherlock Holmes Adventure* by Richard T. Ryan." – Michelle Stanley, Readers' Choice Awards

"All in all, *The Stone of Destiny* is a captivating and intriguing detective novel and another great Sherlock Holmes adventure!" – Caroline Vincent, Bits About Books

"The Druid of Death"

"The clever solution, which echoes one from a golden age classic, is the book's best feature." – Publishers Weekly

"The Druid of Death is clever and fun, a winning combination. The setting — Victorian England — and the Druidic lore are absolutely captivating. This is my favorite kind of mystery." – Criminal Element

" … the Druidic detail and the depiction of 19th-century London are fascinating and delightful." – Kirkus Reviews

"Richard Ryan has found his niche in creating new adventures for our famous detective and his sidekick." – Caroline Vincent, Bits About Books

"The Druid of Death by Richard T. Ryan is a compelling story that transported me back in time and made the iconic duo of Holmes and Watson jump off the page." – Books of All Kinds

"Where many of the tangent series have been challenged to keep these characters [Holmes and Watson} fresh, this author has accomplished not only that but made them enjoyable too." – Jennie Reads

"Ryan creates a thoroughly enjoyable pastiche, giving readers just what you'd expect from such a mystery. The suspense is tangible, and the detection methodologies quirky. He's right on the money with his characterizations of all the usual players, especially Holmes and Watson." – Barbara Searles @thebibliophage.com

"A stunning achievement!" – Ken Bruen, author of *The Guards* and creator of Jack Taylor

"The Merchant of Menace"

Short-listed for the annual Drunken Druid Award.

"Oh, what a joy it is to meet Sherlock Holmes and Dr. Watson again! *The Merchant of Menace* is an exciting adventure of priceless valuables, great detective work and just the kind of devilish adversary we love to read about." – Mattias Boström, author of *From Holmes to Sherlock: The Story of the Men and Women Who Created an Icon*

"This rousing, intriguing, devilishly fun caper, well-executed and well-paced, had me hooked from the first page. The dutiful Watson, Holmes' deductive skills, and a worthy nemesis to rival the evil Moriarty himself, make this cat-and-mouse adventure a page-turning, edge-of-your-seat coaster ride well worth taking." – Tracy Clark, author of *Broken Places* and *Borrowed Time* and the creator of Cass Raines

"[In *The Merchant of Menace*], Ryan takes reality and weaves it together with Sherlockian mythology and a fun mystery." – Barbara Searles @the bibliophage.com

"[*The Merchant of Menace* is] an absolute humdinger of a novel …It is beautifully written, erudite and hugely entertaining." – Ken Bruen, the author of *The Ghosts of Galway* and the creator of Jack Taylor

"*The Merchant of Menace*, Rich Ryan's fourth Holmes novel is his most Sherlockian yet. Moving from what initially seems to be an insignificant incident to a series of crimes with international implications, Ryan presents Holmes the way I like to encounter

him: A true hero who is always three steps ahead of the criminal."
– David Marcum, Sherlockian author, editor and collector

"The wonderfully titled *The Merchant of Menace* has all the familiarity of a lost Holmesian tale. An enjoyable adventure from the ever reliable Richard T Ryan." – The Crime Thriller Hound

"Ryan has a real flair for capturing the language of Holmes and Watson, their foibles, and the dynamics of their relationship. He has created an antagonist and series of crimes that Conan Doyle would have been proud of." – Caramerrollovesbooks blog

"…[Holmes] encounters a rather delicious new 'villain'; this one can give Moriarty a run for his money but instead of trying to one-up the brilliance of Doyle's Moriarty, Ryan pays homage in the making of his 'Merchant.'" – The Caffeinated Reader

"The Case, oh my, the case. This case had Sherlock stunned, but of course that just made our favorite detective work … harder. I love that the more intelligent a criminal, the more respect Sherlock has for them. This case was one of my favorites of all the Sherlock cases. It had suspense, intrigue, and surprise. The entire thing was beautifully written." – Pixie Ponders and Reviews

"With an intriguing premise and a cunning plot, *The Merchant of Menace* will delight Sherlockians of all stripes. Richard T. Ryan has given us a gripping mystery and a loving tribute to the Great Detective." – Daniel Stashower, author of *Teller of Tales: The Life of Arthur Conan Doyle*

Through a Glass Starkly:

A Sherlock Holmes Adventure

By Richard T. Ryan

Hardcover ISBN 978-1-78705-592-6
Paperback ISBN 978-1-78705-593-3
AUK ePub 978-1-78705-594-0
AUK PDF 978-1-78705-595-7

Published by MX Publishing
335 Princess Park Manor, Royal Drive, London, N11 3GX
www.mxpublishing.co.uk

Cover design by Brian Belanger.

As always, this book is
dedicated to my wife, Grace;
as well as my children,
Dr. Kaitlin Ryan-Smith
and Michael Ryan;
my son-in-law, Daniel Smith,
and my granddaughter,
Riley Grace.

It is also dedicated to Russell
Siller, an incredible teacher
and an extraordinary human
being, taken from us too
soon. His influence on me as
a young man cannot be
overstated.

This book is also a thank-you
to all those who have
supported my earlier efforts –
this one's for you!

Introduction

There is a great deal of truth to the old adage: Time flies when you're having fun. When I first came into possession of Dr. Watson's tin dispatch box at an estate auction in Scotland several years ago, I reveled in my good fortune as I devoured the secret trove of untold tales that had fallen into my lap.

As I have indicated in the past, many of the stories had been withheld for personal reasons. Holmes' vanity can be seen as the primary cause for no less than five tales in the box failing to see the light of day.

At the other end of the spectrum, political considerations also played a prominent role in preventing both *The Vatican Cameos* and *The Stone of Destiny* from being published before now.

However, never were such considerations stressed as they were in the tale that Dr. Watson had titled *Through a Glass Starkly*. Given the events that shaped the narrative, it is no wonder the good doctor wished to delay its publication for a very specific period of time. Now that time has passed, and the publication date has arrived.

In what I can only assume is Doctor Watson's hand, a note attached to the first page of the tale makes it clear – without the slightest bit of equivocation – that the manuscript was to be shared with no one but the reader until at least a century and a year had passed since the signing of the Treaty of Versailles, which occurred on June 28, 1919.

I have adhered to Dr. Watson's wishes out of a profound sense of duty to a man for whom the phrase "King and Country" was far more than just words.

Although the events in this tale are now shrouded in the mists of the past, the instructions regarding the disposition of this manuscript were so explicit that to ignore them would have been to do both him and Holmes a grave disservice.

That said, I hope you find the tale as fascinating as I do.

– Richard T. Ryan

Foreword

27 December, 1918

For the last few decades of the 19th century and the first years of the 20th, Europe had been plagued by the incessant sabre-rattling of the old guard. As we moved into the new century, just a few short years ago, I must admit to harboring hopes that the benighted leaders of any number of countries might view the transition as an excuse to turn away from the old hatreds and prejudices and embrace a future that seemed filled with promise.

As I have now come to understand, my optimism was sorely misplaced.

That war was coming was a certainty; it had become merely a question of what the spark would be that ignited the powder keg and set off a conflict that promised to engulf the entire continent. Having been a first-hand witness to the horrors of combat and the misery it spawns, I can assure you no right-thinking man would ever choose that as his first option.

And yet, a never-ending network of secret alliances, backroom deals, jealousy over unchecked imperialism, the rise of *realpolitik* and various other factors all worked in concert to drag us inexorably to the precipice of war. Yet, even in those darkest hours, there were those few men and women struggling valiantly to change the course of that history which too many of our leaders seemed so hell-bent on following. As you know, those noble few were woefully outnumbered and ultimately unsuccessful.

I have long debated whether this story should even be written down, let alone published. Certainly, it serves as a testimony to the remarkable abilities of my friend, Sherlock Holmes, and for that reason alone I have finally decided to set pen to paper. Still, stung as I am by man's utter stupidity and cruelty, I have put in place certain arrangements so as to preclude this tale from being published until at least another century has passed. My hope is that by then man will have learned at least a few lessons from "the war to end all wars," but I must admit I am filled with trepidation.

At any rate, the events in this tale occurred in the late spring and early summer of 1907, shortly after Britain, France and Russia had formed their so-called Triple Entente, the machinations of which had been undertaken in reaction to the Triple Alliance, signed decades earlier between Germany, Austria-Hungary and Italy. Given the fact that Kaiser Wilhelm was Queen Victoria's eldest grandchild, one can but speculate with regard to the animus that must have existed between any number of the European rulers – many of whom were blood relatives – and which resulted in the cataclysm that came to be known as The Great War – as if there could ever be anything great about war.

However, I digress. As the Continent edged towards open conflict, there were those brave men and women, many of whom toiled in anonymity, who sought to halt that unrelenting march towards misery. This is the story of such an effort that was ultimately doomed to failure.

Still, the intent was there, and it was a noble one. Were it not for the actions of a few misguided souls, one can only speculate – a practice of which I am certain Holmes would thoroughly disapprove – how differently things might have turned out on the world stage.

That being said, I now leave to you the tale I have titled "Through a Glass Starkly." I do beg your indulgence, for I must admit to altering a few names and locations in the name of propriety. As for the rest of tale, events unfolded much as I have described.

Had things changed only slightly, the fate of the world might have been quite different, and I fear we are all the sadder for that.

– John H. Watson, M.D.

Anyone who has ever looked into the glazed eyes of a soldier dying on the battlefield will think hard before starting a war.

– Otto von Bismarck

World War I was not inevitable, as many historians say. It could have been avoided, and it was a diplomatically botched negotiation.

– Richard Holbrooke

Chapter 1 – June 1907

It was at the beginning of June in 1907 that Sherlock Holmes sent me a rather cryptic message, indicating he might require my assistance in a matter of some delicacy. I knew that despite his retirement to Sussex a few years earlier to tend to his bees that he had retained the rooms at Baker Street and could be found there occasionally. (Truth be told, I was under the impression he had purchased the lease from Mrs. Hudson and settled a rather handsome annuity on her to remain there.)

In his comminiqué, Holmes had requested that I meet him there on a Sunday night, so we could discuss the matter over dinner – just as we had so many times in our halcyon days. Since my wife was on an extended visit to her family in Scotland, I dispatched an equally cryptic wire to her, instructing her to remain with her relatives until she had heard further from me.

Upon arriving at 221B that Sunday night, Mrs. Hudson greeted me warmly and said, "Mr. Holmes instructed me to give you this as soon as you arrived. I shall have your dinner ready at 6."

I trudged up the stairs to our lodgings, and after settling myself in my favorite chair, which still stood exactly where it always had, I poured myself a brandy and ripped opened the envelope to discover a single sheet of paper bearing a terse message from my old friend.

Watson,

Have been called away on business on a matter of some urgency. I may be gone for a week or more. I am, counting on you to hold down the fort. I will be in touch. Feel free to make the place your own, I am assuming your wife will have no objections.

Sincerely,

S.H.

Initially, it felt quite invigorating to be involved in the hunt once again; however, my enthusiasm soon began to wane after I had neither seen nor heard from Holmes for nearly a week.

Normally, such a prolonged absence would not have overly concerned me, but Holmes had not even bothered to send a wire much less write a letter. While his message had indicated that he expected to be gone for several days, there is still a significant difference between "gone" and totally incommunicado.

And so it was with some relief on that following Saturday evening, I heard his familiar tread on the stairs. I noticed he was ascending quite slowly, and when he finally entered our lodgings, my joy at seeing my old friend was nearly offset by my concern for his appearance.

Always lean, Holmes now looked almost frail. His clothes appeared to hang loosely on his frame, and his face, invariably gaunt, now seemed more lined and sallow then I could ever recall.

I jumped up and said, "Holmes, what on Earth…"

However, he cut me off with a dismissive wave of his hand, and managing a façade of bonhomie, said, "Watson, I cannot tell you how good it is to be home."

"Can I get you anything?"

"I should very much like a brandy," he replied.

"Have you eaten?"

Pausing to consider his answer, he replied, "Not in two or three days, I believe."

"My word!" With that I rang for Mrs. Hudson. Upon entering the sitting room, she took one look at my friend slouched in his chair and said, "I'll be back shortly with some nourishment for Mr. Holmes."

Sipping the brandy that I had given him, I saw Holmes relax somewhat. Although I was curious, I refrained from peppering my friend with all the questions that were dashing about in my head. I knew that he would relate his adventures when he was ready, and there was nothing that could make him speak until that moment.

So we passed the time in a convivial silence. Eventually, Holmes did break the stillness by remarking, "I do hope the bees are faring better than I. My neighbor has agreed to tend to them in my absence." He then relapsed into silence.

Some 20 minutes later Mrs. Hudson knocked on the door and entered with a tray bearing a platter of sliced beef, a bowl of hearty brown gravy and several thick slices of bread, which she placed in front of Holmes.

"I was planning to go to the market tomorrow," she said, "so things are a bit short in the kitchen. If you'd prefer, I can prepare you some eggs and a rasher of bacon."

"No need, Mrs. Hudson," replied Holmes with his mouth already half full. "This is wonderful, but I do hope the eggs and bacon will make their way up here in the morning along with a pot of your best coffee."

"Indeed, they will, sir. And may I say, sir, it's good to have you home."

With that, she curtseyed and left. Had she stayed another few seconds, she might have seen the beginnings of a blush creep into Holmes' cheeks. I watched as he eagerly consumed everything that had been set before him.

I have often remarked about my friend's seeming indifference to sustenance. All I can say, after witnessing Holmes devour the beef and sop up every last bit of gravy with the bread provided, is that every man has his breaking point.

Well-fed and fortified with a second glass of brandy, Holmes settled himself back in his chair and reached for his old clay pipe. I watched as he filled it with shag from the Persian slipper, and a few minutes later it was as though he had never been gone.

After several more minutes had passed, he looked at me and said, "I suppose some sort of explanation is in order."

I merely smiled, and said, "That is entirely up to you."

He nodded and then began, "You know the state of affairs in Europe at the present."

"All too well, I'm afraid."

"At this very moment, there is another Peace Conference being held in The Hague. The heads of state of several nations are hoping to reach an accord regarding the conduct of war. As I am sure you will recall, this second conference in The Hague had originally been scheduled for 1904, but had to be postponed due to the outbreak of hostilities between Russia and Japan."

"How ironic that a peace conference should be delayed because war had broken out."

Holmes cast a wry look in my direction. "Indeed," was all he said.

"As a result of the Russo-Japanese conflict, the Japanese have emerged as a force with which to be reckoned on the world stage."

"True," I said, "Russia had every opportunity to save face and bring the war to an early resolution, but convinced of its superiority, it pressed on and suffered a number of humiliating defeats. Still, what has all of this to do with you?"

"I have often spoken of the power my brother wields within the government."

"Unless, I am mistaken, you once remarked of Mycroft that, 'Occasionally he *is* the British government,' adding that at times, he is 'the most indispensable man in the country.'"

"Bravo, Watson! Well, this is one of those times. Mycroft hand-picked the delegates to the peace conference, and he has been in constant contact with one or another of them since they departed for the Netherlands."

"My word!"

"Yes, apparently shortly after they had left, my brother learned that an attempt would be made on the life of one of the French representatives, and all the evidence would point to the German delegation."

"But to what end?"

"To stoke the fires of hostility and to push Europe still closer to the precipice of war and quite possibly over the edge."

"But if the Germans were not the ones making the attempt, then who was it?"

"That is where things get murky," said Holmes. "Mycroft had been provided with a code name for the assassin, Atlas, but little else. He immediately made me aware of the problem and tasked me with foiling any assassination attempt. He wanted me to travel to The Hague and serve as a sort of bodyguard for the French.

"I explained that it would be impossible for a single man to guard the entire delegation as it was highly unlikely the members would constantly be in each other's company – both day and night.

"Mycroft understood that but insisted he wanted me on the scene, so that when he learned the identity of the would-be assassin, he would already have a man in place. He also told me that everything I was doing was top-secret."

"So that explains why I didn't hear from you."

"I'm afraid my hands were tied," said Holmes, who then continued, "I arrived in The Hague six days ago and found a cable waiting for me at my hotel."

"Had Mycroft learned the real name of the assassin?"

"He had but rather than risk putting it in a telegram, he sent me a clue."

"What on Earth do you mean?"

"The telegram contained but a few words *'Flambe pied-à-terre.'*"

Although my French is poor, I was still able to translate that phrase without difficulty. "A flaming apartment? What on Earth was Mycroft thinking?"

"Actually, Mycroft was being quite clever, and banking on the fact that I would be up to the task."

"So you were able to discern some secret meaning in his rather mysterious message?"

"Indeed. The fact that he had written the text in French had me thinking of that country immediately. Apparently, Mycroft had become aware of the fact that the assassination attempt would actually take place in Paris rather than The Hague. I immediately boarded a train for that city, and some fifteen hours later I arrived at the Gare du Nord."

"And the flambe pied-a-terre?"

"You still haven't figured that out? Although many Parisians are aware of its existence, I am not certain how far that little secret has spread in the rest of the world."

"Dash it all, Holmes. Can you not come to the point? What secret?"

"When Monsieur Eiffel constructed his tower, he also had built a small apartment for himself near the top."

"My word! Well, that explains the inclusion of the phrase pied-à-terre, but surely it was not on fire?"

"No," Holmes laughed. "You correctly translated the word *flambe* as flames, or as we would say 'burning.' However, Mycroft required an extra layer of deception in case the cable should happen to be read by the wrong eyes, so he dropped the last 'e' from *flambée*, which we can also translate as 'exploding' or 'soaring,' usually with regard to prices, hence the idiom *la flambée des prix.*

"I must confess it took me some few minutes to figure out my brother's intent, but once I divined his meaning, I understood he wanted me to find a 'soaring apartment.' Fortunately, I knew of one, and as it is located in Paris, I believed it to be the only one that fit Mycroft's description."

"So you headed to the Eiffel Tower?"

"Yes. When I arrived, there was a man standing near the base of the tower. I recognized him immediately even though he was doing his best to appear inconspicuous. Apparently, he also was acquainted with me because he approached me and said, "Monsieur Holmes, I have been waiting more than a day for you. I was beginning to wonder if perhaps something had happened to you."

"I smiled and apologized for any inconvenience I might have caused him."

"'Think nothing of it,'" he said. 'I have been requested to give you these,'" he said, handing me an envelope. 'Now, if you will excuse me, I think my work here is complete. I am leaving tomorrow for Greece, and I shall be gone for at least a month.'"

"What was in the envelope, Holmes?"

"A letter, which I could produce in case my presence in the apartment were questioned, and a set of keys."

"You don't mean…"

"I'm afraid, I do. Gustave Eiffel had just turned over the most exclusive residence in the City of Lights to me."

"But why?"

"I rather suspect in some capacity Eiffel is in league with Mycroft. Be that as it may, I was more interested in what I might find in the *'flambée pied-à-terre.'*"

"And what did you discover?" I asked.

"After ascending nearly to the top of the tower, I made my way to the apartment which I entered to discover a fully stocked wine cellar, including some excellent vintages, as well as a cabinet generously stocked with provisions – and another missive from my brother."

"And what did Mycroft's letter say?"

"The assassin had been positively identified as an Austrian nationalist named Stefan Lorenz. Mycroft said he had other agents trying to learn anything they could about Lorenz.

"According to my brother, Lorenz is a former soldier who was dispatched to China in 1900 as part of the multi-national force sent to quell the Boxer rebellion. He seems to have been quite the military man, reveling in the plunder and bloodletting that followed the Siege of the Legations in Peking. Once he was separated from the military, he became a soldier-of-fortune and eventually began to hire himself out as an assassin.

"Although there was no photo of Lorenz, something that did not totally surprise me, there was a rather detailed description which was actually quite pointless, for in the last line of the account, he was described as a master of disguise."

"Sounds rather familiar," I grumbled.

Holmes looked at me and then grinned, "Yes, in a very real sense, I suppose you could say I was hunting myself. I had just finished perusing Mycroft's letter for a second time, which also instructed me to make the apartment my base of operations while I remained in Paris. At that point I looked over and noticed something laying on the floor. Apparently, it had been slipped under the door.

"It was another letter, but when I opened the door to see who might have left it, there was no one there. The only person in sight was a young woman just entering the lift to descend.

"A woman, you say?"

"Yes, I can only assume it was she who had delivered the letter. Since pursuit was pointless, I returned to the apartment."

"What did the letter say?"

"Here. You may read it yourself." With that Holmes pulled a sheet of paper from his jacket pocket and handed it to me.

After I had unfolded it, I saw a single line of gentle cursive in an obviously feminine hand. I read it over three times, looking for clues, and then I turned to Holmes. "What does it mean?"

"I think it means exactly what it says:

'Lorenz uses a crutch.'"

Chapter 2

Holmes continued, "The next morning, I made my way to the *Élysée Palais*, where the Council of Ministers was holding regular meetings with President Fallieres. After each session, they would dispatch various junior secretaries to The Hague with instructions for the delegates.

"As you know the *Élysée Palais* is located near the *Champs Élysées* in the 8th Arrondissement. I made my way there in an effort to determine the lay of the land. I had no intention other than to familiarize myself with the area and the buildings that house the French government. I walked along the Quai d'Orsay, crossing the Seine at the Pont de l'Alma. As I am sure you are aware, the bridge was named to commemorate the 1851 victory in which the Ottoman-Franco-British alliance defeated the Russian army in the Crimean War.

"Even though I am not the least superstitious, I took it as an omen, if you will, that once again the British and French were joining forces against a common enemy."

"And well you should, old man. That was a grand victory, but it came at a dreadful price, with more than

8,000 brave men on both sides dead at the end of the day." For a moment, I reflected on my days in Afghanistan, and when I returned my gaze to Holmes, I could see he knew exactly what I had been thinking.

Holmes continued, "Once I had crossed the bridge, I proceeded up the Avenue Montaigne to the Rue du Faubourg Saint-Honoré. As I drew closer to the *Palais,* I was looking for anyone who might be using a crutch. I saw two men, but in both cases they appeared to be missing a leg. While that didn't eliminate them totally, it did raise questions in my mind about Lorenz and the crutch.

"However, I also noticed a beggar with his cap on the ground in front of him, sitting near one of the columns not too far from the main gate. I watched as several people dropped coins into the wretch's hat as they passed. Apprising him a bit more carefully, I noticed that although both legs appeared sturdy, there was a rather odd-looking crutch leaning against the wall behind him.

"Feeling that if he were not Lorenz, he might prove an invaluable ally, I fished a few centimes from my pocket and tossed them into his cap as I strolled by. I must admit to being rather surprised when he failed to respond in any way. He was wearing tinted glasses, and

I wondered whether he might have fallen asleep. As I stood there, with just a few passersby in the vicinity, I noticed something white in his cap where I had tossed the coins. I glanced at it rather furtively and saw that it was a note addressed to me."

"To you? How is that possible?"

"I am still trying to ascertain that, Watson. When I was certain no one was about, I retrieved the note."

"What did it say Holmes?"

Holmes then pulled a second paper from the inside of his coat and handed it to me. After I had unfolded it, I saw in printed letters, "You need not concern yourself with Lorenz any longer. Now, remove yourself from the game."

"My word, Holmes. Were you able to glean anything from the note?"

"Only that it was written by a man. Given the final phrase and the strong character of the penmanship, I should say the author is educated and perhaps with a military background. The paper is common foolscap and the ink tells me nothing."

"Well with Lorenz dead, how did you come to be in the state that you are in?"

Smiling ruefully, Holmes said, "That is where things begin to get interesting. As you might imagine, I wanted nothing more than to examine the body. There were no outward signs of violence that I could see and no blood on the ground, so I walked to the corner, waited a bit, and returned a few minutes later. There were still just a few passersby, none of whom attracted my attention.

"Striking up a conversation with the dead man, I bent down to see if I might smell any type of strange odor on the body or emanating from the lips, and as I did I heard a sudden clang, Looking up, I saw a knife bounce off the stone wall directly in front of me. Had I remained standing, I have no doubt the blade would have been embedded in my back or neck.

"Snatching the knife, I looked around, but as you might expect, there was no one to be seen who might have thrown the blade. Since I had no idea of their numbers, I set off on foot, always keeping a wary eye out for possible pursuers. I was loath to return to the Eiffel Tower, so I headed for the Gare d'Orsay and purchased a ticket for Orleans. After making certain that I had not been followed, I disembarked two stops later and hired a carriage to take me to the Théâtre de la Gaîté-Montparnasse on the Rue de la Gaîté, in the 14th Arrondissement.

"Prevailing upon an old friend at the theatre, I was soon disguised as a sailor, complete with a full-beard and eye-patch. I then returned to the *Élysée Palais*, but the body had obviously been discovered and removed. Not knowing where to turn nor whom I could trust, I headed for the Pigalle section, where one might find any number of disreputables. Despite buying more glasses of wine than I care to remember, information about Lorenz proved to be a rare commodity.

"Later that night, or perhaps I should say early the next morning, I returned to the Eiffel Tower. Once in the apartment, I studied the knife carefully. It was a beautiful piece of work, Watson. Perfectly balanced, it was a single piece of steel with no grip on the handle and a blade so sharp that any surgeon in Europe would have few qualms about using it in place of a scalpel."

"My word, Holmes. It sounds like quite a nasty bit of work. Do you still possess it?"

"Unfortunately not. I was forced to part with it in order to effect my escape from a rather large ruffian who was pursuing me at the time."

Chapter 3

"In retrospect, it would appear I had not been as subtle in my questioning at the various establishments as I had thought. Someone had apparently caught onto me, and I was followed when I left Pigalle. After I had eluded my pursuers, I returned to the Tower, as I said, and doffed my disguise. I changed my appearance again as best I could under the circumstances. I then made my way to the Gare du Nord. I had considered sending Mycroft a wire, but in the end, decided it would be best to report to him in person.

"Having learned my lesson from my encounter with Lorenz, I decided to reconnoiter the station on the chance there might be people there in anticipation of my arrival. Taking stock of my surroundings, I discovered four men waiting at the station. They were fairly easy to spot, and I may someday set pen to paper to compose a monograph about the fine art of loitering inconspicuously."

"Holmes, you spotted four men, and you knew that all four were waiting for you? How on Earth?"

"They had arranged themselves on various platforms around the trains departing for Dover, each one covering a corner of the station. This way, were one to spot me, they could all converge rather quickly."

"But how did you spot them? And more to the point, how did you elude them?"

"On my way to the station, I had purchased a beret, several books, a few of which I secured with a belt, and an umbrella. I must have looked half-daft. After all, I was fumbling with and dropping my books and carrying this large blue umbrella on a brilliantly sunny day. I also made no effort to conceal my presence – hiding, as it were, right in front of them.

"Although I was certain they were there for me, I still had to prove my supposition. Two of the men were holding newspapers which they were not even pretending to read; moreover, they were both smokers, and I readily observed several cigarette butts near the feet of each. Obviously, they had been waiting there for some time."

"And the other two?"

"The third one was equally easy to spot as he had a flask with him, and I observed him drinking from it on three separate occasions."

"And the last one?"

"He was the easiest of all to spot. Although I must confess it required very little deduction."

"How so?"

"He was a mirror image of the second man I had located. They were certainly brothers and quite possibly twins."

"Having located them, what did you do next?"

"I walked up to the last one and handed him a note I had written beforehand. I told him a man at the other end of the station had asked me to deliver it."

"What did the note say?"

"The note said simply: 'Holmes wearing bowler, blue jacket, boarding train to Boulogne-sur-Mer.' He immediately started running for that track, yelling to his companions and pointing to the engine, which was just pulling out of the station. As you might expect, they were desperate to board that train – and they succeeded."

"And you?"

"I waited until the train had departed with them on it, then I booked passage to Dunkirk. From there, I crossed the Channel and made my way to Dover where I boarded a train to Victoria. During the time I was gone, I had slept little and eaten less, and I fear it took its toll on me. However, I am feeling much more like myself now, and should like nothing more than a good night's sleep in my own bed and a hearty breakfast."

"But Holmes, you were sent to foil an assassination attempt."

"Yes, and for some inexplicable reason, someone did my job for me. As a result, the questions now are who and why, but enough of that. A pipe before bed?"

"Holmes, you just told me how you eluded the lookouts in Paris, but earlier you said that you had to use the knife thrown at you to escape from a rather sizable ruffian."

"And so I did. Upon my arrived in Dunkirk, I made my way to the ferry where I observed an extremely large man who had taken up a position just a few feet from the base of the gangplank. He was closely inspecting everyone boarding the boat, and I saw him interrogate two different gentlemen. Although I was disguised, they must have described my overall appearance, including my height. I remained concealed until just moments before the ferry was scheduled to depart. I was rather hoping, he would abandon his post as the ship prepared to set sail, but no such luck.

"Deciding I needed a diversion, I stood up and yelled, 'I believe you are looking for me?' As he sprinted towards me, I ran around a pile of crates, planning to double-back and beat him to the gangplank.

"What I hadn't reckoned on was a man of his size moving with such speed. He was in hot pursuit and gaining on me as I sprinted towards the boat, so I did the only thing I could do, I drew the knife, turned and threw it at him."

"You didn't kill him, did you?"

"No, Watson, but I fear he will be walking with a limp for the foreseeable future – if not permanently. As you are aware, I am somewhat proficient with knives, and I aimed for his right leg and caught him just so. The blade did most of the work, and he went down like a felled tree."

"So then what do you plan to do next?"

"I have been asked to meet with Mycroft tomorrow night at the Diogenes Club. I do not think he would have any objections were you to accompany me."

"I will be there," I promised.

"Excellent. Let's dine at six and, weather permitting, stroll to the Diogenes while enjoying a cigar on the way."

The next morning, I arose before Holmes and waited for him before I sat down to breakfast. Normally, an early riser, he appeared just after nine and looked refreshed and revitalized. "Solid food and a good night's rest, just what the doctor ordered," I thought. As Holmes and I breakfasted together, he once again attacked his food with a fervor I had seldom seen in all our years together.

"For whom are you covering today?" he asked, a twinkle in his eye.

"Up to your old tricks now that you are feeling better? Should I even bother to ask?"

"Watson, you are a creature of habit. When you are serving as a locum, you inevitably rise early and prepare your bag, so that should a sudden emergency arise, you are ready to deal with it immediately."

Pointing with a piece of toast he had slathered with marmalade, he continued, "There is your bag by the door – as though you might forget it – so I repeat: For whom are you covering today?"

I told Holmes that I was holding office hours for my friend Dr. Burton, who had been covering for me but had been called away due to a death in the family. As I departed, I saw my friend, a self-satisfied smile playing across his face, reaching for the papers.

After an uneventful day, I returned to Baker Street. As Holmes and I dined, I found myself unable to avoid the obvious. "Any news from France?"

Holmes chuckled, "I was wondering when you would get around to it.

"To answer your question, yes. There have been a few developments. According to a letter I received from Mycroft, Lorenz was hired by a group of Austrian agitators. Apparently, they are hoping if a war should break out, they would find themselves allied with Germany and, in the event of a victory, be allowed to join the North German Confederation."

As Holmes had paused, I added, "I never understood why Bismarck acted as he did in excluding them. Left to their own devices, they have pursued gains in the Balkans and become little more than an *agent provocateur* on the world stage."

"Europe is an arsenal, Watson, and each country a veritable powder keg. The slightest spark, whether in the form of an attack or something as simple as a perceived slight of some sort, may ignite a blast that will in turn trigger other explosions. I have no idea who or what may survive such a cataclysm. However, I do know that we must strive to make certain that the first spark never catches. Now, shall we see what Mycroft has to say?"

When we stepped outside of 221B, the evening was so pleasant that we followed up on our earlier plans and walked to the Diogenes, enjoying a cigar as we strolled.

The warm weather and long day had brought the city to life in the early evening. Street vendors were hawking an array of items, and the sidewalks were crowded with people enjoying themselves in anticipation of the next day that promised more fine weather.

When we arrived at the Diogenes, we were ushered into the Stranger's Room, the only place in that most unusual club where conversation is permitted. After a few moments, Mycroft Holmes entered the room. Rotund, Mycroft looked drawn and tired as he eased his considerable bulk into a wing chair that faced us.

Looking over at me, Mycroft began, "I hope you will not think me rude, Doctor, but there is a matter of some urgency which I must discuss with my brother. If you would excuse us for just a few minutes, you may take a seat in the club, and I will have a valet attend to your needs."

As I rose to leave the room, Holmes said, "Anything you wish to say to me, you may say in front of Doctor Watson. He is the very soul of discretion, as I am sure you are aware."

I turned to Holmes and said, "It is quite all right. I shall just enjoy a whiskey and soda while you two discuss … whatever it is Mycroft wishes to discuss."

As Mycroft started to thank me, Holmes rose from his seat and said, "I believe we have no further business here, Watson."

"Sherlock, be reasonable," said Mycroft. "These are matters that concern princes and potentates. The very future of Europe may, in some small measure, be determined by what course of action we decide to pursue here this evening."

"All the more reason for Watson to be a part of it. He brings a perspective to such matters that you lack and to which I find myself indifferent."

Seeing that his brother refused to be swayed, Mycroft picked up a small silver bell and rang it. When the valet appeared, he said, "Please bring us three whiskeys and a gasogene. Thank you."

When the valet had departed, Mycroft looked at Holmes and said, "You acquitted yourself well in Paris."

Barely acknowledging the compliment, Holmes said, "Kind of you to say so, but I fear I cannot agree. In my own defense, I can only argue I lacked the time and the resources to conduct a proper investigation."

"I meant by escaping the followers of Lorenz. Apparently, they were told you had poisoned him and were determined to exact their pound of flesh, as it were."

"Who gave them my name? And how did they become aware of my presence in the city?"

"We are seeking the answers to those very questions. Were I to hazard a guess, I would say someone in our government let the cat out of the bag."

"You mean to say I was betrayed by someone working for you?" Holmes asked incredulously.

"As much as it pains me to admit it," replied Mycroft.

"We are entering an age where information has evolved into a type of currency. If you know two companies are planning to merge, you can buy stock in advance and realize enormous profits.

"In a somewhat similar way, if you know two countries plan to sign a treaty…"

"Yes, yes. I understand," said Holmes, cutting Mycroft off. "But what has all this to do with the peace conference in The Hague and the attempted assassination of a French official?"

"What I am about to tell you is a matter of national security, and must not be repeated under any circumstance." Looking at me, Mycroft said, "You have been forewarned. Doctor, are you still certain you would like to remain?"

"He is staying," replied Holmes. "In the past, he has proven himself invaluable to me, and I am certain that he will demonstrate his mettle once again, many times over."

"Very well, then," said Mycroft. "What would you say if I were to tell you that for all intents and purposes the peace conference in The Hague is nothing more than an elaborate distraction?"

Chapter 4

"A distraction?" I asked. "Pray tell, from what?"

"The delegates now meeting at The Hague are discussing an array of topics, including naval warfare, the rules of war, the treatment of prisoners and the obligation of neutrals," said Mycroft. "Do you notice anything missing?"

"Will they take up the potential causes of the next war, or are they treating it as a *fait accompli*?" asked Holmes.

"And there you have it," replied Mycroft. "Each and every country appears to be operating on the assumption that another war is inevitable. And while that may well be the case, I refuse to accept it as the first premise."

"So you are going to look at war logically?" asked Holmes.

"Is there any other way to examine it?" his brother replied evenly.

"You still haven't answered my question," I interrupted. "A distraction from what?"

"It's actually quite simple, Doctor. While those meeting in The Hague prattle on about the conduct of war, I am planning to hold a top-secret conference with a few highly placed officials from various nations in an effort to circumvent another conflict.

"Given everything that has transpired in Europe and elsewhere over the past half century, my fear is that the next war will not be limited to hostilities between two or three nations. Rather, I am inclined to believe that while it may well begin that way, as alliances are brought to bear on both sides of the conflict, we could easily end up witnessing a display of unchecked aggression that may well engulf the entire continent. When Canada joins the fray, as it no doubt will, it may well have a domino effect on such nations as America and Japan. Should they become involved, as well as the various African colonies, the war may well place the whole world at odds."

Recalling the horrors I had seen in Afghanistan, I found the notion of the entire globe at war both shocking and repugnant. "You cannot be serious."

"I fear brother Mycroft makes a point that will be difficult to argue with," said Holmes, suddenly rejoining the conversation. "We have already seen one attempt to thwart the peace effort in The Hague. It is impossible to say how many other groups out there are all too willing to 'Cry havoc and let slip the dogs of war.'"

"And so you see my problem," said Mycroft. "My little gathering must remain completely under wraps. The fewer who know about it, the better for all involved."

"And what would you have us do?" asked Holmes.

"You have a network that is unique," replied Mycroft. "I would imagine there is little that transpires in this vast metropolis about which you do not know or could not learn, should you so desire."

"I should say so," I replied. "Between his contacts, on both sides of the law, as well his contingent of Irregulars, there is precious little that transpires throughout this great city that escapes your brother's attention."

"I am counting on just that fact," replied Mycroft. "In your writings, Doctor Watson, you have described me as having – what were the exact words?" He paused here for just a second, "Ah, I have it – 'no ambition and no energy.'"

Before I could say anything in my own defense, Mycroft continued, "Tut, Doctor, I take no offense. For while your description of my rather sedentary nature is most assuredly accurate, you have also done me the great honor of praising my mind in a rather fulsome manner. I believe 'omniscience' was the term you had my brother utter in characterizing me."

He smiled and said, "Like my brother, I too possess a certain sense of vanity."

As you might expect, I was dumfounded by Mycroft's remarks. I had no idea that he had read my works, let alone remembered them with such amazing accuracy. Looking about the room, I happened to notice a rather dated edition of *Cassell's* on the table as well as several newspapers and a few other periodicals, hidden beneath the dailies. However, as far as I was able to ascertain, there were no copies of *The Strand* in the room.

I sat there in silence and then Mycroft said, "Another quality I share with my brother, is that I, too, am a voracious reader."

I was thinking to myself, physical dissimilarities aside, the Holmes brothers really are quite alike – more so than they might realize. Almost on cue, Mycroft looked at me and said, "After all, Doctor, as I have said, we are brothers."

As I sat there marveling at Mycroft's words, I found myself wondering if the elder Holmes might have any adventures worthy of publication which he might be willing to share with me. All of a sudden, my thoughts were interrupted when Mycroft said, "I am sorry, Doctor Watson, but I am afraid all of my tales must remain confidential."

"Am I that transparent?" I asked incredulously. "I won't even ask how you deduced what I was thinking. I have seen your brother do it on countless occasions, and yet I am still amazed when it happens."

"In this case, it was rather easy," said Mycroft. "You seemed taken aback when I referenced your literary endeavors. As you sat there, trying to collect your thoughts, your eyes wandered to the table laden with reading matter. You spotted the copy of *Cassell's* that contains a story by Henry Rider Haggard, and I should think the rest is obvious."

"Remind me never to play cards with either of you," I said.

My feeble joke elicited no response from either Holmes brother, so I lapsed into silence.

Sherlock Holmes broke the quiet when he asked, "When will this conference of yours take place?"

"Right now, it is in the planning stage," Mycroft replied, "but I am hoping to have everything in place within a fortnight – three weeks at the most – and then perhaps two or three days after that, to allow for travel from the Continent."

"So you are not planning on including the Americans?"

"Initially, I think not. Perhaps if things go well, and those on hand are able to arrive at a consensus, we may well send an envoy to President Roosevelt. After all, he was one of the driving forces behind the gathering in The Hague."

"I should think you would want to engage them as soon as possible," I said.

"I fear that would be getting ahead of ourselves. I should much prefer to present President Roosevelt with a carefully formulated plan of action rather than have him and his Rough Riders further muddying waters that I am certain are going to appear quite murky at the beginning."

"So, what exactly is it you wish me to do?" reiterated Holmes.

"I wish I could be more precise, but as I stated, I want you to employ your vast army of informants to keep you apprised of any unusual activities they may encounter. Ask them to pay particular attention to anything that may involve foreigners."

"I usually offer the Irregulars some sort of recompense," said Holmes.

"A practice I should wish you to continue," said Mycroft. He then withdrew his wallet from his jacket pocket, counted off several notes and handed them to Holmes. "Pay them at your usual rate, and offer a bonus to anyone who brings you information upon which we can act.

"As for yourselves, go about your business as usual, but do be careful. As I have suggested, we may well have someone in our own government working at cross-purposes with us. As we get closer to the conference, I shall be in touch, and if you should hear of anything unusual, please make me aware of it at once."

As we were walking home, I said to Holmes, "How concerned do you think we need be?"

Rather than answering me, Holmes surreptitiously raised a finger to his lips, indicating I should remain silent. We had been strolling along at a leisurely pace, but it wasn't until we reached the hustle and bustle of Oxford Street that Holmes abruptly changed course and headed up Duke Street towards Manchester Square.

"Once around the park, I think," he said as we approached the small island of green. At that point Holmes finally looked at me and said, "We were being followed back there. I have no idea whether it was one of Mycroft's people checking up on us or someone else entirely. At any rate, I shouldn't be surprised if a different pursuer picks up our trail on the other side of the park."

"Surely you jest, Holmes. Why in heaven's name would anyone follow us?"

"Consider where and with whom you have been tonight and what you have learned. I am certain there are people who would pay large sums of money for that information.

"Now, let us keep our eyes peeled as we return to our lodgings."

I was still pondering what Holmes had said as we continued along Fitzhardinge Street after exiting the park. We had walked perhaps two hundred feet when Holmes gently nudged me with his elbow and discreetly gestured across the street where a man stood gazing in the window of one of the fashionable homes.

I nodded to show that I understood. As you might expect, the man kept his distance, but we were aware of him, and it was with some relief that we finally entered the front door of 221B and ascended to our rooms.

"Who do you suppose that was?"

"I should think it was one of Mycroft's minions, no doubt assigned to watch over us now that we have been drawn into my brother's rather elaborate scheme."

"Will you be able to function with someone constantly looking over your shoulder?"

"Absolutely not," replied Holmes firmly, "and I will write to Mycroft first thing in the morning to say that I find the situation both invasive and intolerable. If he wants my help, he will have to accept it on my terms. Now, Watson, what say you to a pipe and a brandy before bed?"

I was awakened early the next morning and was summoned to a medical emergency. The local constable, believing I was the closest physician, had sent for me to assist with a woman who had gone into labor unexpectedly. As I departed, I thought a saw a man loitering on the other side of Baker Street, but he didn't follow me. After delivering the infant, I returned to our rooms and a discreet glance, as I entered our lodgings, showed that the man was no longer present. Feeling exuberant but ravenous, I bounded up the stairs where I found Holmes sitting in his chair, perusing the papers.

"So was it a boy or a girl?" he asked from behind the paper.

"A girl," I replied absentmindedly, and then it hit me, "How could you possibly know what I have been doing?"

"There are several clues that give you away. First, you entered the room carrying your bag and with a slight smile on your face. Obviously an indication of some success at a medical endeavor. Second, your clothes are hardly rumpled, although I believe I can detect a faint spot of blood on your right cuff. Finally, there is just the slightest hint of a sweet smell in the air, either ether or chloroform, although I am inclined to believe you employed the latter."

"Holmes, is there no end to your wizardry?"

"And the mother? She is well too, I assume."

"Yes, mother and daughter are doing fine. And may I ask how your morning has been? Are you still planning to write to your brother?"

"I already have, and the situation has been remedied," he said with a grin.

"So those were his people last night?"

"He wanted to make certain we arrived home safely. I informed him that if he did not call off the watchdogs, he would have to seek help in another quarter. Now Watson, you must be famished.

"After you have eaten, I should like to pay a call on Lestrade."

"Has this anything to do with last night?"

"Perhaps," he said enigmatically. He then rang the bell and some ten or fifteen minutes later, Mrs. Hudson delivered a plate piled high with poached eggs, toast and bacon as well as a fresh pot of coffee. I was just pouring myself a second cup when the doorbell sounded, and a minute later, I heard Mrs. Hudson exclaim, "Wait a minute, young man!"

Suddenly, a wild-haired young man burst into our sitting room. He looked first at me and then Holmes and then he rushed to my friend and said, "Mr. Holmes, you must help me."

"I tried to stop him, Mr. Holmes," said Mrs. Hudson from the doorway.

"And I appreciate the effort," replied Holmes, "but I am certain this fellow means us no harm. Thank you, Mrs. Hudson."

My friend then turned and, looking at the man, said serenely, "I am Sherlock Holmes, as you correctly surmised, and you are?"

"I am Neville Barrett, and unless you help me, I am ruined."

"Do compose yourself, Mr. Barrett. Would you care for coffee? When you are ready, please begin at the beginning."

I poured the young man a cup of coffee to which he added two lumps of sugar. I noticed that his hand appeared to be visibly shaking as he brought the cup to his lips. "I really shouldn't be drinking this," he protested.

After finally getting some of the coffee down, Barrett began his story. "I work at the British Museum."

"Ah," I said, interrupting him, "Then you are no doubt acquainted with our good friend, Dr. Steven Smith"

"Indeed," said Barrett, "It was Dr. Smith who sent me to fetch you."

"What on Earth for?" inquired Holmes.

"He told me to tell you that *Cotton Vitellius A XV* has been stolen. And he asked that you come to the Museum as soon as possible."

Holmes sat bolt upright, "The *Southwick Codex* has gone missing. Return to the Museum directly, and inform Dr. Smith I shall be there as soon as possible."

For the first time, I saw a bit of relief on the lad's face as he said, "Thank you, Mr. Holmes." After professing his gratitude to Holmes several more times, he said he would notify Dr. Smith that we would be along directly.

After he had departed, I said, "While it was obvious that you knew to what the lad was referring, I must confess to being totally in the dark."

"'The *Southwick Codex*' is something of a misnomer in that it also contains the far more valuable *Nowell Codex*. Between them, the two books, which have been bound as one, contain among other things Old English adaptations of Augustine of Hippo and the Gospel of Nicodemus."

"I grant you they may well be important manuscripts, but are they really that valuable?"

"I have not finished, Watson. In the *Nowell Codex* you will find a homily on St. Christopher as well as the only existing copy of *Beowulf*."

"My word, Holmes!"

"It's true, Watson. *Beowulf* survives in but a single copy that was believed to have been written sometime around the end of the tenth century."

"But what was all that Cotton Vitellius nonsense that Barrett mentioned?"

"When Henry VIII dissolved the monasteries in the middle of the 16th century, Sir Robert Cotton collected and bound more than a hundred volumes of records and papers. In his home, he fashioned a library that he organized in a unique manner."

"Do tell," said I, now genuinely interested.

"On top of each bookcase in his library was the bust of an historical figure, including such luminaries as Augustus Caesar, Cleopatra, Julius Caesar, Nero, Otho, and Vespasian. All told, there were, I believe, 14 busts – the 12 Caesars as well as Cleopatra and Faustina the Younger, the wife of Marcus Aurelius. He then gave each shelf a letter designation, with A being the top and F being the bottom, and then he numbered the books from left to right. So his system involved knowing the name of the figure on top of the case, the shelf letter and the volume number.

"Although he had a great many priceless manuscripts, including two copies of the Magna Carta, the most famous among the manuscripts came to be known simply as '*Cotton Vitellius A XV*' and '*Cotton Nero A X*.'"

"Well, now that I know that Vitellius refers to the *Beowulf* book, what was the Nero manuscript?"

"*Cotton Nero A X* contains all the works of 'The Pearl' poet. In fact, as you might have surmised, the manuscripts are still known by those call numbers in the British Library. Now, let me dash off a note to Lestrade, and while I'm doing that, why don't you hail us a cab?"

I went downstairs and quickly secured a hansom. Holmes and the page came out together, and as the youngster sprinted down the street, Holmes climbed into the cab. He instructed the driver to take us to the British Museum.

Perhaps fifteen minutes later, we stopped in front of the museum and were striding across the courtyard when Dr. Smith came running out to meet us. We had worked with him on two previous cases, which I have titled *The Druid of Death* and *The Merchant of Menace*, and I believe Holmes may have consulted with him on a number of other occasions.

Normally poised and the picture of equanimity, Smith looked distraught. "Mr. Holmes, I cannot thank you enough for coming so quickly."

"Let us adjourn to the privacy of your office," said Holmes, "and you can tell me exactly what happened."

After we had walked to Smith's office, which was located on the lower level, Holmes said, "Now, begin at the beginning. Please omit nothing. Even the most seemingly insignificant details may play a large role in such a case as this."

Smith began by saying, "I think a little background might be in order, just to underscore the gravity of the theft. The Cotton library was willed to the British nation in 1700 and the manuscripts were eventually moved to Ashburnham House where they were kept in storage. In 1731, a fire broke out at Ashburnham. Some manuscripts were lost forever and others, including a copy of the Magna Carta with the Great Seal affixed, were damaged beyond repair. Fortunately, the *Beowulf* manuscript was only singed along the edges of some its pages.

"When the British Museum was founded in 1753, what remained of the collection, including the *Nowell Codex*, passed into its hands. Sadly, the manuscript has not always received the care that it deserves. Despite it being one of a kind, the book appears to have been carelessly handled in the museum's earliest years.

"Fortunately, a Danish scholar, G.J. Thorkelin, had made two copies of the manuscript in 1787, else we might have gaps in the poem due to the damage. Thorkelin also published the first printed edition of *Beowulf*. Finally, in 1845, the Museum mounted each leaf on a paper frame and rebound the manuscript. However, as you might expect, it remains extremely fragile and must be handled with the utmost care. It has remained safe in the rare book room until just recently."

"When did you last see the book?" asked Holmes.

"I had occasion to be in the rare book room about a week ago," said Smith. "Whenever I find myself there, I inevitably look at the *Beowulf* manuscript and a few others."

"So as near as you can tell, that book may have been stolen a week ago?"

"Not quite," replied Smith. "I sent Mr. Barrett to the room on Friday morning, and he will swear that it was there at that time."

"Much better," exclaimed Holmes. "So we now know the manuscript was taken within the past 72 hours.

"And was the rare book room closed this past weekend?" asked Holmes.

"Yes. Although, we will open it occasionally to accommodate a scholar visiting from abroad, we have had no such requests recently."

"So there were no scholars here this weekend?"

"No," replied Smith.

"So then exactly who, aside from visitors, is working in the Museum on those days?"

"We have our usual complement of security guards and perhaps a dozen docents," replied Smith. "However, there is always a guard of some sort outside the rare book room – seven days a week. They confiscate all parcels as none are allowed in the room, and whenever someone leaves, he inspects their case if they have one."

"Are they competent?" asked Holmes.

"Silas Green, who works during the week, is a pensioner," replied Smith, "who previously worked as a constable. He did so much volunteer work here that we decided to put him on the payroll. But to answer your question, I would say that he is more than competent. He takes his duties quite seriously and is both punctual and diligent. He checks everyone going into the room, but more importantly, he checks everyone leaving the room – and quite thoroughly, I might add. Since he has assumed his new position, we have yet to lose anything from the rare book room."

"And who works the weekends?"

"We have a number of volunteers, but this weekend, it was young Mister Barrett who volunteered to work both days. He is writing a book and the shift is a quiet one."

"He seems like a dependable chap," observed Holmes.

"He has been with me for four years now, and his work is exemplary."

"Have you had problems with books going missing in the past?" asked Holmes.

"I believe in the past, one or two collectors may have absent-mindedly taken a book or two home," remarked Smith.

"You are too kind," said Holmes. "These books are all quite valuable, are they not? So if one were to substitute 'deliberately' for 'absent-mindedly' it would be easy to see why you felt a guard was necessary."

I smiled inwardly, thinking tact never had been Holmes' strong suit.

At that point, Holmes looked at me and shrugged his shoulders, as if in resignation. "I should very much like to interview this Mr. Green at some point as well as Mr. Barrett," said Holmes. "Is Green around?"

"Unfortunately, he is off today – a death in the family. But if you will just tell me when you would like to speak with him, I will make certain that he is available."

Holmes nodded and then changing tack, asked, "How did you come to learn that the manuscript was missing?"

"This note was on my desk when I arrived at work this morning," said Smith, handing Holmes a single sheet of white paper.

Tasking it from Dr. Smith, Holmes read it and then passed it to me. In a gentle cursive that seemed vaguely familiar, it read:

If you wish to see
Cotton Vitellius A XV again,
do not contact the police. We
will be in touch.

P.S.: Since I know you
will be in touch with him,
please give my regards to
Mr. Holmes.

Chapter 5

"My word, Holmes. That sounds exactly like …"

"Your so-called 'Merchant of Menace'," he replied finishing my sentence for me. "Indeed, it does," he continued, "I have often wondered if we should ever hear from Mr. Bullard again."

"You don't mean that fellow who tried to steal the Tara Brooch several years ago?" asked Smith.

Holmes had first encountered Charles Bullard, an American criminal who had been forced to move to England, in the adventure I had titled *The Merchant of Menace*. A master thief, who specialized in stealing rare antiquities for wealthy collectors, Bullard had been apprehended while trying to purloin a priceless Faberge egg from the Duchess of Marlborough at her country estate, Blenheim Palace. Bullard had been spared the gallows and sentenced to life in prison after providing the names of several individuals who had retained his services. He subsequently escaped from prison and had not been heard from since that time.

"The *Beowulf* manuscript certainly seems like the type of item that might interest him," I said.

"Indeed, it does," replied Holmes, "and the note certainly seems to hark back to our earlier meetings."

"Gentlemen," said Dr. Smith, "I don't mean to interrupt, but I would beg that you do everything in your power to recover the *Codex*. When you consider all that it has been through, the survival of the *Beowulf* manuscript might be considered nothing less than a miracle. Somehow, it defied the destruction of pagan poetry which occurred after the rise of Christianity in the Middle Ages. Despite the dissolution of English monasteries, it managed to remain intact. Though damaged by fire in 1731, and buffeted by the winds of deterioration and neglect, it has survived. Whether you want to call it luck or see the hand of Divine Providence in its preservation, this seminal piece of Old English literature has been passed on to the present day. You must secure its return so that not only our generation but future generations of students and scholars will be able to study and enjoy it."

I know I was touched by Smith's rousing appeal, and I believe Holmes was as well. However, never one to wear his heart on his sleeve, my friend simply replied, "I promise you I will do everything in my power to see that *Cotton Vitellius A XV* is returned to you."

Holmes then asked to see where the manuscript had been kept. Smith led us to The King's Library in the East Wing. He stopped in front of a heavy oak door with four small windows in it. Sitting in the hall were a desk and a chair.

"Normally, that is where Mr. Green, sits," offered Smith by way of explanation. "Barrett was filling in until I dispatched him to summon you."

"Just so," replied Holmes, giving the furniture a cursory glance.

Withdrawing a ring of keys from his pocket, Dr. Smith opened the door and led us into a back room.

"The public is not allowed here," explained Smith. "Scholars wishing to examine the manuscripts must make an appointment, and then they are permitted in the room alone although there is almost always someone with them in case they should require assistance of any kind. The guard locks them in and then opens the door when they wish to leave."

"So they are unsupervised while in the room?" observed Holmes.

"We are not talking about children, Mr. Holmes, but serious scholars."

Looking at me, Holmes shook his head almost imperceptibly and then turning to Smith, he asked, "Were there any appointments made on Friday?"

"Yes, there were a total of four. I have noted the names and addresses of the visitors. Three of them are well known to me and the fourth is an academic with impeccable credentials from Heidelberg University in Germany," said Smith as he handed the paper to Holmes. After examining it, Holmes thrust it into his coat pocket.

"Have you any idea what the German was researching?" asked Holmes.

"I believe he was trying to authenticate a rare first edition of Dr. Johnson's Dictionary, which had copious markings and notes in the margins. He believed many of them were in Johnson's hand."

"So then you saw the book?" asked Holmes.

"Yes, he arrived at the museum shortly before we closed on Thursday, the week before last. He apparently was under the impression we remained open late that day. After introducing himself and showing me the book and the notes, I suggested he return the next day when he could spend the entire morning and the afternoon, if need be, comparing versions."

"And did he?"

"He was quite punctual and returned precisely at ten the next morning and remained until sometime late in the afternoon. I can check to see exactly what time he left if you like. His research apparently continued into last week for he was here every day."

"That won't be necessary," my friend replied. "Did Mr. Green examine his bags and books each day?"

"I cannot say for certain, but knowing Silas as I do, I should think everything was checked every day – and quite carefully."

At that point, we had arrived in a corner of the room, "This is where we keep the oldest and rarest manuscripts. Pointing to a glass-topped case, he continued, "That was where the *Beowulf* manuscript was displayed."

Holmes examined the oak cabinet, which appeared solid and formidable. He then dropped to one knee and, pulling his lens from his pocket, began to consider the lock carefully. When he had finished, he turned to us and said, "There are a few discernable scratches of recent vintage, but I cannot say for certain whether they were made by a lock pick or someone with a shaky hand and a key."

"There are but three keys to that display, Mr. Holmes. I have one. There is an extra one stored in a safe in the security office, and the third is kept in another safe in the director's office."

"Wasn't Bullard a safecracker of some renown?" I asked.

"Indeed he was," replied Holmes, "which leads us to the obvious question: Have the other two keys been accounted for?"

"Before you arrived, I checked with both security and the director, under the pretext of possibly changing several locks. In both instances, the key was exactly where it was supposed to be."

At that point, Holmes appeared to return to his examination and suddenly lifted the top of the display case up.

"How on Earth?" exclaimed Smith.

"I must tell you," said Holmes, "while those locks appear formidable they would offer little challenge to anyone with even the slightest skill with a lock pick."

"I shall have them changed immediately," said Smith.

"Better late than never, I suppose. Still, you have delivered me a pretty little problem, Dr. Smith. Rest assured, I shall give it my undivided attention."

"Mr. Holmes, I cannot thank you enough."

At that point, Holmes began to examine the nearby shelves and display cases. Smith and I looked at each other, and I gave him a knowing glance. At one point, I heard Holmes utter what I can describe only as a grunt of surprise.

After several more minutes, Holmes turned to Smith and said, "You will keep me abreast of any and all developments?"

"You may count on me," said Smith.

During the cab ride back to Baker Street, neither of us spoke. Holmes, I knew, was ruminating on everything he had just learned. I had my own concerns but I am certain they were of a very different ilk from my friend's. When we had finally reached our lodgings and settled ourselves in the sitting room, Holmes looked at me and simply asked, "What's bothering you, Watson?"

"You just told Dr. Smith, you would give this case your full attention."

"Indeed, I did."

"How can you possibly work on the theft of the *Beowulf* manuscript and keep your word to your brother?"

"Mycroft seeks information. The Irregulars and my other informants will be keeping an eye out for anything out of the ordinary, and they will immediately apprise me of anything they might happen to discover."

"Yes, and what if they come seeking you while you are out chasing down a clue about the *Beowulf* problem? Not even Sherlock Holmes can be in two places at one time."

"Well, then my friend, it appears I am going to require the assistance of a good second at all phases of these cases. Are you up to the task?"

"You can depend on me, Holmes."

"I knew I could. Now, let us have a talk with Wiggins and see if he can find the time to help us with our quest."

Although he had grown into a strapping young man, Wiggins remained as devoted to Holmes as he always had been. I wasn't quite certain what Wiggins did to earn his bread and cheese, and, truth be told, I wasn't sure I really wanted to know.

Holmes simply let one of the urchins who could always be found within the environs of 221B know that he wished to see Wiggins, and an hour later, I heard the front bell ring. A few minutes later, Wiggins, who was now as tall as Holmes and just as slender, knocked on the door, and my friend bade him enter.

"It has been a while, Wiggins," said Holmes.

"I am always at your service, Mister 'Olmes," replied Wiggins warmly.

Holmes then explained to Wiggins what he wanted him and the other Irregulars to do. He finished by saying, "I wish I could be more specific, but no one knows where the threat may come from nor what form it may take. In fact, we cannot be absolutely certain that there will be a threat."

"So, you're telling us to be on the lookout for anything that seems a bit," he hesitated as if searching for the exact right word and finally finished with "peculiar? Especially if it involves foreigners? Is that it?"

"Exactly," said Holmes. "The usual wages will apply. Should you or one of your mates come across anything unusual – anything at all – I want you to report to me as soon as possible, no matter what the hour may be."

"You're making this sound more mysterious than usual, Mr. 'Olmes, but we'll do our best."

"That's all anyone can ask of you, Wiggins," said Holmes.

After Wiggins had departed, I once again tried to sway Holmes. "You know there is a big difference between having the Irregulars report to you and keeping an eye on the situation yourself."

To which Holmes replied, "I know you think I am shirking my duty, but whatever happens with regard to Mycroft's secret conference would, in all probability, have its genesis with a report from one of my street Arabs. Since they outnumber me by a large margin, I shall devote my attention to the one case where I believe I can make a difference rather than trying to be everywhere at once and thus totally ineffective."

I could see the point to Holmes' logic, and I also understood it was fruitless to argue with him, so reluctantly I decided to let the matter drop.

Taking my silence for acquiescence, Holmes then said, "I am going out to make some inquiries, and I may be gone for several hours. You may accompany me, or you may remain here on the off chance that one of the Irregulars has something to report. In which case, you can contact Mycroft, either at his office or at the Diogenes Club. It is entirely your choice."

Since I still harbored a thought that Holmes was abrogating his duty to his brother, I decided to remain at Baker Street. I am willing to admit that the fact that I was still a bit chafed at my friend might have contributed to my decision.

Left to my own devices, I managed to catch up on my correspondence, which I had neglected for several days. I was just beginning to transcribe my notes from one of our recent cases, when I heard his familiar tread on the stairs.

Looking at my watch, I realized that it was half past five and nearing supper time. When Holmes entered, the look on his face spoke volumes.

Throwing caution to the wind, I decided to beard the lion in his den: "How was your afternoon?"

"Rather curious," he replied.

"Oh?" I inquired.

"I have contacted several individuals, on both sides of the law, and no one was even aware that *Cotton Vitellius A XV* had gone missing."

"And you find that odd?"

"Perhaps. Since no one has heard of the theft, I find it reasonable to conclude the only two people involved were the buyer and the thief."

"It does rather recall the Merchant," I offered.

"Agreed, so either I have not yet contacted the right person, or there is another element at play in the theft."

"How will you ever find the buyer? It could be anyone."

"Actually, no. Would you be interested in owning an Old English manuscript?"

"I wouldn't know what to do with it," I replied.

"Neither would the overwhelming majority of people living in England," said Holmes. "The people who could afford to pay for such a theft are a very small subset, and within that group, I would be willing to wager there are just a few that have any interest in *Beowulf.* So you see, Watson, the pool in which I am searching is quite shallow and not very large at all."

"It could be a foreigner," I offered.

"Considering the linguistic background of *Beowulf*, it very well could be a Dane or some other individual of Scandinavian heritage. For that matter, it could be someone of Germanic extraction, but I think we can safely dismiss the Italians, the French, the Russians and any number of other nationalities as well. You may have increased the possibilities, but I am inclined to think the buyer is of English stock.

"It just remains for me to locate the proverbial needle in the haystack, but I am persistent, a fact to which I believe you will attest."

I nodded my assent, so Holmes continued, "And despite your protestations, I really do believe that I am dealing with an incredibly small sheaf. Now, do I smell shepherd's pie or is my nose failing me as well?"

"Mrs. Hudson told me that she would be preparing something special, so I am inclined to trust your sense of smell, old friend."

Our landlady delivered a savory feast which Holmes and I both relished. After the meal, we enjoyed brandy and a cigar. All told, it was a thoroughly pleasant evening until it was interrupted by the unexpected arrival of Inspector Lestrade. Mrs. Hudson announced him, and the little man strode into our rooms – the picture of agitation.

"Mr. Holmes, I am in desperate need of your help."

Holmes bade the Inspector sit and then poured him a brandy.

Unable to contain my curiosity any longer, I asked, "Lestrade, what is wrong?"

"One of our informants tipped us off to a smuggling ring, operating down on the docks.

"I took a half-dozen good men, but when we burst into the warehouse, it was completely empty. There was no one there, nor were there any smuggled goods. As we were searching the premises, one of the constables entered what appeared to be an office."

"And what did he find?" asked Holmes.

"There was a large desk in the middle of the room, and the constable set about searching it. There was the usual assortment of papers and other office paraphernalia that you might expect. However, in pulling out one of the drawers, he noticed that it seemed too short for the space allotted to it in the desk.

"After measuring the draw and then the desk, he noticed there was a difference of some six inches."

"He sounds like a very sharp officer," I observed.

Ignoring my remark, Lestrade continued, "Upon looking more carefully, he soon discovered a secret compartment concealed by the drawer. After locating the hidden spring, he managed to open it."

"And pray tell, what did he find?" asked Holmes.

"He said the only thing inside was a single key."

"Was there a safe in the office?" asked Holmes.

"Indeed there was," replied Lestrade. "The officer tried to open the safe using the key he had found in the drawer."

"And he was successful?" asked my friend.

"He was," replied Lestrade.

"Out with it man," cried Holmes. "Must I drag every last detail from you?"

"I know how you like to be thorough," replied the Inspector. "At any rate, after he opened the safe, the only thing inside was a large envelope, addressed to me.

Inside the envelope there were notes, totaling perhaps a thousand pounds."

"Yes, but such a mundane discovery would not bring you to my door at this hour. What else did he discover?"

"You are right, Mr. Holmes. There was also a note among the money."

"And what did it say?

"It read: *'Lestrade, here is your share.'*"

Chapter 6

"Surely you jest!" I exclaimed.

"I wish I were kidding, Dr. Watson, but it's true. As a result, I have been suspended, pending an official investigation."

Holmes suddenly cleared his throat, and both Lestrade and I turned to look at him. "Of course, I will help you, Inspector. Now, as you are familiar with my methods, please begin at the beginning."

"We first began hearing rumors of a large smuggling operation in late February and early March, but back then, that's all they were – rumors."

"From whom did you hear these rumors?"

"They came from a number of sources. As you might expect, most of the men giving us information were thimble-riggers, wires and others of that ilk."

I must have appeared totally befuddled, for Lestrade looked at me and taking stock of my obvious confusion, said, "I must admit I am rather surprised, Doctor. Given your long association with Mr. Holmes, I would have thought you would be more conversant with criminal slang."

Holmes chuckled, "Watson is a literary man, Inspector. I am afraid the local underworld patois has yet to find its way onto his pages."

"My apologies, Doctor," said Lestrade. "A thimble-rigger is a man who runs a deceitful game of chance, such as the shell game, usually in the street."

"And a wire?"

"A wire is a pickpocket with extraordinarily long fingers," added Holmes.

He then continued, "Inspector, did it not strike anyone as odd that a number of low-level thieves and tricksters were privy to the operations of what was purported to be a rather sizable, and dare I say lucrative, smuggling ring?"

"Now that you put it like that, yes. It does seem rather queer – in retrospect."

"Were you given any information about the types of goods being smuggled?"

"On more than one occasion, we were told that the gang was bringing in high-quality spirits from the Netherlands and France."

"Well, that might explain it," I suggested. "Perhaps they were going to employ these men to deliver the product for them. After all, if the buyers never saw the seller, they could not testify against them if it should ever come came to that."

"You do make an interesting point, Watson; however, I am rather more inclined to think there was another motive for bringing such mundane thieves into their confidence."

"And that would be?" asked Lestrade.

"In due time, Inspector. I am developing a theory, and I have not all the pieces in place to support it just yet. At any rate, Lestrade, what was the impetus behind the raid?"

"The rumors persisted, and one of the local restaurant owners, whose brother is also an inspector, informed him that he had been offered cases of Bordeaux and Chardonnay for half of what he had been paying. He suspected something was fishy. Apparently, he's been losing business because other places have cut their prices on the spirits."

"Of course," said Holmes. "Pray continue."

"He began buying small quantities, and we eventually followed one of the deliverymen back to the warehouse. We tried to get one of our men hired as a laborer but without much success, so my superiors authorized the raid on the warehouse which we carried out earlier this evening. However, when we arrived, the warehouse was empty. No workers, no wine, no paperwork – only that damned note in the safe."

After a pause, he looked at my friend and asked, "So what am I to do then, Mr. Holmes?"

"You are to go home. Enjoy the time off that has been allotted you and trust in me to see you through this."

I could see that Lestrade had been hoping for something more than mere reassurances from Holmes, but he had learned over the years that my friend's word was his bond.

After the Inspector had taken his leave, I looked at Holmes and said, "I hope you are not taking on too much."

"What on Earth do you mean?"

"You have promised to help your brother, a task which you have assigned to me on a *pro tempore* basis. You have sworn to help recover the *Beowulf* manuscript and now you have added aiding Lestrade to the list of tasks you must accomplish. I would remind you that, despite your uncanny abilities, you are flesh and blood and require rest and sustenance, just as the rest of us mere mortals do."

"Watson," he exclaimed, "I am in my element. This is what I live for, what I was born to do, my *raison d'etre*. Vexing as they may appear, these problems are not insoluble, and they are certainly not to be feared, old friend. Rather, they should be relished."

I could see there was no dissuading Holmes from the Herculean tasks that he had set himself, but I promised myself that I would be more vigilant regarding matters of his health and stamina – concerns to which I knew he would not give a second thought.

Holmes spent the rest of the evening poring over his scrapbooks and when I finally retired a bit later, he was still at it.

I awoke the next day to discover that my friend had already breakfasted and departed. With little to do but wait to hear from the Irregulars, I spent the morning transcribing the notes from one of our earlier cases, a particularly unusual affair I had decided to title, "The Adventure of the Ruined Ritual."

The case had occurred about a year prior. Holmes and I had been enjoying a week in the country when one morning we were hastily summoned to a nearby estate –

propriety forbids me from revealing the name of the family or the location until a great many more years have passed. The estate's owner had been found dead in his library, which had been locked from the inside. There were no signs of foul play, and although a number of people stood to profit handsomely from his death, none had been near the house for several days. As you might expect, the members of the local constabulary were totally baffled.

After interviewing the household staff, Holmes learned that the victim had been behaving erratically for several days prior to his demise. I suggested that perhaps his behavior had been brought about because the man possessed an impending sense of doom. As you might expect, Holmes merely scoffed at that notion and dismissed it straightaway. Later that morning we visited several shops in the village and after hearing one of the shopkeepers remark that the man had acted as "mad as a hatter" the last time he had been in his establishment, I supposed that Holmes was correct in dismissing my rather fanciful notion.

After a visit to the local police station, Holmes insisted we return to the library immediately. As we entered, the maid was leaving the room carrying the tea set on a tray. I was rather surprised when Holmes inquired if she might prepare tea for the two of us.

Apparently the body had just been removed an hour or so previously, and she had finally been allowed to resume her duties.

During her absence, Holmes conducted a thorough examination of the room. At one point, I heard him mutter, "Just as I suspected," as I saw him struggling to open a rather recalcitrant window.

A few minutes later, the maid returned with our tea, and Holmes excused himself to wash his hands. When he returned, he was carrying a copper teapot in his hand. He looked at the maid and asked, "Would you mind brewing our tea in this kettle? I am rather partial to tea that is allowed to steep in a pot like this. It is much favored by our landlady, and I have developed a fondness for it."

She bowed and said, "Certainly, sir." She then left the room. A few minutes later, I heard yelling and cursing, and I wondered at the commotion. I dashed outside to find one of the local constables holding the maid while the sergeant was about to remove the top from the teapot to peer inside. Before he could, Holmes, using his walking stick, knocked it from his hand. "Forgive me Sergeant, but that is one pot which I believe you do not want to examine too closely. In fact, unless I miss my guess, you were holding the murder weapon."

"This" said the sergeant, picking up the pot by its handle but holding it at arm's length. "I do believe you are pulling my leg, Mr. Holmes."

"I assure you I am quite serious," replied my friend. "In fact, I have no doubt that when you have that teapot tested, you will find traces of mercury in it. I believe that Miss Hagstrom here was using the mercury to slowly poison her employer. The fumes from the metal would account for his rather eccentric behavior of late, and I am certain that she just kept adding small doses to the pot every time she prepared his tea. What he didn't ingest, eventually evaporated and the fumes merely helped speed the process along."

Later, I said to Holmes, "That was a rather clever deduction on your part."

"Clever," he scoffed, "not at all Watson. I have been far too slow on this case."

"What on Earth do you mean?"

"I can claim no credit for the solution," he stated.

"If not you, then who?"

"The offhand remark by the shopkeeper, do you recall it?'

"I believe he said something about the victim having bats in the belfry."

"Not exactly, old friend. His words were the victim seemed 'mad as a hatter.'"

At that point, my medical training kicked in, "So you suspected that he had been exposed to mercury as the cause of his erratic behavior. But how did you come to suspect the maid."

"He lived there all alone, except for the staff. When we returned to the house, I saw the maid bringing out the tea service. I noticed she was carrying the copper teapot, yet when she returned a few minutes later with our tea, it had been steeped in a china pot. Why employ a second teapot? In the interval, I discovered that the one window in the library was impossible to open because two slender finishing nails had been driven into the frame. All she had to do was serve the tea and close the door. Between what he ingested and what he inhaled, his demise was all but assured."

"But why, Holmes?"

"I rather suspect Miss Hagstrom was designated in the will for a fairly significant bequest, but I shouldn't be surprised to learn that she was working in concert with another of the heirs, who promised her ample compensation in return for her assistance."

The transcribing filled most of my morning and afternoon. There was no word from the Irregulars nor did I hear from Holmes. Finally, around five, a note arrived addressed to Holmes. When he finally returned some three-quarters of an hour later, he looked dispirited. He entered his bedroom and returned having donned his blue dressing gown. He then filled his pipe with shag and collapsed into his favorite chair.

"I am guessing there was no news," I ventured.

"Is it that obvious?" he asked, smiling.

"An educated guess," I said.

"You know how I feel about guessing of any kind," he said. "Sadly, today was one of the least productive days I have experienced in quite some time. I made a number of discreet inquiries, or had others make them for me, and surprisingly, no one appears to know anything about the *Beowulf* manuscript or Lestrade's smuggling ring. I don't suppose you have heard anything from the Irregulars?"

"Not a word, and I have been home the entire day."

"Which adventure are you writing up now?"

"And you know I spent the day writing, how?"

"The coffee pot is on your desk; the pile of books next to it is unmoved, and your inkwell is nearly dry. I looked as I walked by. Child's play, really."

"Holmes, you are incorrigible," and then remembering the note, I reached into my pocket and said, "This arrived for you about an hour ago."

Opening the letter, he perused it and looking at me said, "Mycroft would like us to meet him in his office, tomorrow morning at ten. Can you make it?"

"Certainly," I replied. "I should like nothing more than to escape these rooms for a while."

Holmes then wrote a short note and summoned the page. "Please deliver this to my brother at the Diogenes Club." After the boy had departed, he looked at me and said, "I do hope that Mrs. Hudson has something substantial planned for supper. I am rather hungry."

He need not have worried, as she had prepared a succulent trout with roasted potatoes and leeks. After dinner, we chatted a bit and then Holmes set about perusing his year-books while I decided to visit my club.

The next morning, we enjoyed a hearty breakfast and at 9:30 were safely ensconced in a hansom on our way to Whitehall. Mycroft's office is located not all that far from the Diogenes Club in a rather non-descript building. We spent a few minutes waiting in a drab outer room before being led into Mycroft's inner sanctum by a fellow who had introduced himself only as Geoffrey.

Sitting on a large chair that bore more than a slight resemblance to a throne, Mycroft held court from behind a massive oak desk that had been polished to a brilliant sheen. The elder Holmes' considerable bulk seemed normal in a room where all the furnishings appeared oversized.

"Have you any news for me?" asked Mycroft. "Has your army of minions heard any rumblings of which I should be aware?"

"Not that I know of," replied Sherlock.

"Well, I have a bit of news for you," he replied. Looking at me, he said, "Dr. Watson, conversations in this room are sacrosanct. I trust I may rely upon your discretion?"

"Certainly," I replied.

"The peace conference I am planning is now something of a misnomer. Given a few recent developments on the Continent, I have decided I must now make certain the Empire has allies upon whom she may depend when – not if, for I am now certain it will – war breaks out.

"I will be meeting with emissaries from Russia and France. As you might expect, given our recent history, the negotiations with the French will be extremely delicate. Those with Russia, I hope, will be less so, considering the blood ties that we share."

"But we share similar ties with Germany," I protested.

"Yes, but we no longer have Bismarck to keep the Kaiser in check," replied Mycroft. "Left to his own devices, Kaiser Wilhelm has charted what he calls 'A New Course' for his nation, He hopes to cement Germany's status as a world power. Sadly, I fear Europe may well be the worse for it.

"At any rate, I was hoping to hold our meetings in the British Museum…"

"The Museum?" Holmes asked.

"I thought my visitors might pose as tourists, and we might retire to one of the more remote conference rooms to conduct our business. A few Russians and

Frenchmen visiting our great repository of treasures, what could be more natural?"

"What dissuaded you?" inquired my friend.

"The sudden disappearance of *Cotton Vitellius A XV*. If the museum staff cannot secure something that precious, how can I depend upon them to guarantee the safety of my visitors?"

"I won't even ask how you came to be aware of that fact," said Holmes.

"Nor should you," replied Mycroft.

"So where will you hold your meetings?"

"I was thinking we might commandeer the Marble Arch for a few days."

"Brilliant," I exclaimed. "Another popular sight that tourists visit and you should have plenty of police officers on hand there as well."

"My thoughts exactly," replied Mycroft. "I cannot stress the importance of these meetings," he continued. "So brother, do keep your ear to the ground and if any of your street Arabs should stumble across anything unusual or untoward, please inform either myself or Geoffrey."

"Of course," replied my friend.

As we rose to take our leave, Mycroft said, "One more thing. I have heard of the sudden difficulty in which your friend, Lestrade, finds himself. I am certain that you are going to endeavor to clear his name, and I commend you for your loyalty. However, I feel equally compelled to remind you that my planned conference must take precedence as your primary focus – not Lestrade and certainly not the *Cotton Vitellius A XV* manuscript. I trust I have made myself quite clear."

I saw Holmes bristle and redden ever so slightly, but he quickly regained his composure and turning to Mycroft said simply, "For King and Country."

As we turned once more to leave, I heard Mycroft say, "I do hope that was not merely a show for my benefit. For if such is the case, it was a most unconvincing one."

Outside in the hall, Holmes said nothing, but I could tell that he was still angry. As we left the building, I gave some consideration to attempting a conversation but then thought better of it. As you might expect, the ride back to Baker Street was a quiet one.

It was only after we had ascended the stairs and settled into our respective chairs that Holmes looked at me and said with an air of detachment, "Of course, Mycroft is correct. So I must parcel my time most judiciously. I have two friends in dire straits, but how do we balance the career of a single man and the loss of a manuscript, albeit a priceless one, against the possibility of a continent, and possibly the world, engulfed in war and the thousands, no millions, of deaths that may result should anything derail Mycroft's conference?"

"It is certainly no easy task that has been placed before you, yet if there is one man capable of pulling it off, I believe that it is you."

Holmes smiled at me briefly, and then repeated the oft-heard refrain, "Good old Watson."

Had I known the enormous strain my friend would be forced to endure, the degree to which he would exert himself, and the toll that his labors would take upon him, I am not certain I would have encouraged him in any way.

Chapter 7

The next morning I was joined at breakfast by a former Jack-tar, who had obviously seen better days. Sporting a soiled seaman's blouse that had been patched in several places, a disreputable hat, worn trousers and shoes that were down at heel, Holmes looked sorely out of place as he took the chair opposite mine. Truth be told, with his lank hair, darkened skin and blackened teeth, I was quite glad that our landlady had deposited the tray and departed before my friend made his appearance.

"I take it you are investigating Lestrade's smuggling ring."

"I thought I would visit the docks and see what, if anything, people working there might have learned about the smugglers. I am also planning to check up on the Irregulars to see if they have discovered anything untoward during their reconnaissance that might affect Mycroft's conference."

"So two cases at once," I laughed.

"A happy confluence," replied Holmes.

"Is there anything I can do to facilitate your investigations?"

"Do you remember Madame Isabella Cocilovo-Kozzi?"

"The bookseller who helped us with the Tara Brooch? How could I forget! What a striking woman."

"Yes," said Holmes, as though he had not even heard me.

"I seem to recall you describing her as more concerned with the spirit of the law than the letter."

Holmes looked at me curiously, "Watson, I will never take your measure. If memory serves, those were pretty much the self-same words I used to sum up *one* aspect of her personality."

"Is she also an expert on manuscripts?"

"No, but her husband is. I stopped by there yesterday to see if he knew anything at all about the missing *Nowell Codex,* but the shop was closed. You might recall they are located in Bedford Square. Look sharp or you will miss it. Shall we meet back here for dinner?"

"Excellent, and then we can exchange information," I said pointedly, hoping Holmes would dispense with his usual reticence.

"We shall see," he replied.

After breakfast, Holmes left through the rear of Baker Street while I went out the front door. Hailing a cab, I directed the driver to take me to the British Museum. I called upon Dr. Smith, who informed me that nothing further had been heard about the missing manuscript. He had received no communication and, as Holmes had requested, said nothing to anyone, not even his superiors. He then asked me, "Has Mr. Holmes made any progress?"

Deciding a small white lie might prove more comforting than the unvarnished truth, I replied, "He is working on it as we speak. He is pursuing a different angle."

My fib seemed to ease Dr. Smith's anxiety, and he left me feeling slightly better than when we had met. Upon leaving the Museum, I crossed over to Bedford Square. I walked along a row of well-kept Georgian houses, and was surprised to see a small sign in one of the windows, bearing the legend "Rare Books."

I rang the bell, and after a short wait, Madame Cocilovo-Kozzi answered it herself. "Why Dr. Watson, what a pleasure to see you again."

I was a bit taken aback as we had only met on one occasion, "You remember me?" I asked.

"Of course," she replied pleasantly. "We crossed paths at the British Museum when I delivered the Tara Brooch."

"That's a rare gift," I observed.

"Thank you," she replied. "It certainly comes in handy when trying to remember the particulars of any given book. Now, what can I do for you and Mr. Holmes?"

"Actually," I replied, "Mr. Holmes suggested that I speak with your husband."

"A question about a manuscript then. Hold on, let me just call him." She then led me into a sitting room that was filled from floor to ceiling with bookshelves and books. While she was in the hall calling upstairs to "Jonathan," I was wandering about the room where a number of titles caught my eye, including bound editions of both *The Faerie Queen* as well as a copy of *Gulliver's Travels*.

When she entered the room a moment later, I asked, "Are those originals?"

"Of course," she replied. "This *is* a rare book shop." Following my glance, she added, "Spenser oversaw the printing of his own work while we believe this 1735 edition of Gulliver's Travels to be the *Edito Princeps* of that particular work."

At that moment, we were joined by a thin, angular man, perhaps my height, with piercing hazel eyes and a mane of silver hair, whom Madame Cocilovo-Kozzi introduced as her husband, Jonathan.

After pleasantries had been exchanged, he began the conversation by asking, "How may I be of assistance to you and Mr. Holmes?"

"What I am about to tell you must remain within the confines of this room," I cautioned them.

After they had agreed, I informed them about the missing *Beowulf* manuscript. Although they seemed surprised by my news, they both remained silent, allowing me to finish. I concluded by looking at Jonathan and saying, "Mr. Holmes has informed me that your particular area of expertise is manuscripts, and he wonders if you might have heard of any offers to sell the *Cotton Vitellius A XV*."

"To say I am taken aback by your news would be an understatement," Jonathan began. "The *Beowulf* manuscript is a national treasure. As a scholar I have been privileged to examine it on several occasions – none recently. If it has been taken, it is in serious danger."

"How so?" I asked.

"The museum has learned from its past mistakes and now treats these manuscripts with the appropriate degree of care. That is why I said I have not seen it recently. I can only hope that whoever purloined it knows how to handle such a fragile specimen."

He continued, "Bear with me a minute, Doctor." I watched as he walked confidently between two shelves and returned carrying a large wooden box. Placing it on the table, he opened it. Inside was a well-worn, oversized page, perhaps 14 by 9 inches, covered with characters from a language with which I was not familiar.

Looking at me, Jonathan explained, "This is a page from *The Red Book of Hergest*. Written in Welsh in 1382, it is regarded by some as the most important manuscript in the medieval period. Although that is not an opinion I am inclined to share, its importance cannot be overestimated. This manuscript takes its name from the rather distinctive color of its leather binding, but I digress.

"This was written hundreds of years after the *Beowulf* manuscript, and you can see the perilous state of the skin."

"Skin?" I interrupted him.

"The *Beowulf* manuscript was written on vellum, as is this page, which is actually calfskin. At the time, it was considered the premier medium on which to write. Other skins and membranes were also used, but vellum was generally employed for important documents, including the Magna Carta. Thus unless it is being properly cared for, the *Beowulf* manuscript is in grave danger. Tell Mr. Holmes that he may rest assured I will do everything in my power to locate it, but I am not optimistic."

"Why do you say that?"

"If the manuscript were available, I believe I should certainly have heard of it," he gave me a rather cynical smile before adding, "As a result, I am inclined to think that whoever has made off with the manuscript was either hired to do so, or the thief is also a collector. In any event, the fact that word has not spread about its availability compels me to think a collector either stole it or commissioned the theft."

I left the bookshop uncertain of what to feel, but I thought Holmes would find Cocilovo-Kozzi's assessment, if nothing else, interesting.

I returned to Baker Street, and spent some time pondering how I might help Lestrade. I knew that the other two matters were out of my depth, but I felt that there must be some way that I could be of assistance to the inspector.

As I sat in my chair mulling things over, I heard the bell ring. A minute or so later, Mrs. Hudson knocked on the door. "Beggin' your pardon, Doctor. There is a young woman at the door who insists upon seeing Mr. Holmes."

"Holmes is not here," I replied, "and I don't expect him until at least dinner time, possibly later."

"She seems quite distraught, Doctor. Perhaps you would be kind enough to have a word with her?"

"Very well, if she is content to see Holmes' second, then by all means show her up. However, please advise her that Mr. Holmes is quite busy at the moment.

If she will not be put off, then I suppose I will have to stand in for my friend."

In no time at all, Mrs. Hudson had ushered a smartly dressed young woman into the sitting room. With her long auburn hair, brilliant blue eyes and porcelain-like complexion, she was quite stunning. Taking stock of her attire, I noticed that her emerald costume was of the finest brocade, and the pin she wore also appeared quite costly. Having risen, I crossed to her, extended my hand and said, "I am Dr. John Watson. I believe Mrs. Hudson has informed you that Mr. Holmes is not at home at present, so how may I be of service?"

At that she began to sob, I led her to a chair and did my best to comfort her. After a moment, I rang the bell. When Mrs. Hudson knocked, I gave the woman a moment to compose herself as I requested a pot of tea from my landlady.

When I returned to her, she had gathered herself a bit and began by saying, "My name is Deborah Werth from Shrewsbury in Shropshire, and you must think me an incredibly silly woman. Truth be told, Doctor, I am desperate." With that pronouncement, she began to sob softly into her handkerchief.

"There, there, my dear. Tell me what the problem is, and I should think that Mr. Holmes and I may be able to provide some sort of remedy."

"I am in fear for my life," she confessed. "I have only recently wed, much to the chagrin of my family, and now I believe my husband is trying to kill me."

"My word! But why, my dear? If you are recently married, I would assume that you were happy – at least during your courtship."

"We were extremely happy until our wedding night, and then everything changed. George was suddenly a different person. I felt as though I no longer knew the man I had married."

"And you say this happened in one night?"

"Yes, Doctor."

At that point, I went downstairs to see what the delay was with the tea, and when I returned, just a few moments later, she was gone. Needless to say I was baffled by this sudden turn of events. I ran into the street, but there was no sign of her. When I returned inside, I found Mrs. Hudson ascending the stairs with the tea. I explained what had happened, and she continued up the stairs, saying I could probably do with a cup.

Mystified, I followed her and resolved to tell Holmes everything that had occurred.

A few hours later, I heard the front door open and close, and a few seconds later I heard my friend's tread as he ascended the stairs. He entered, looking a bit grimier than he had in the morning. I said, "By the looks of it, you have had a difficult day."

"Difficult, no," he replied. "I would be more inclined to call it informative. Still, it must pale by comparison to your encounter with a member of the fairer sex."

"How the deuce could you know that?" I demanded.

Looking at me, Holmes continued unperturbed, "Reddish hair, petite, quite attractive," pausing for effect, he added, "and she departed rather suddenly."

"Holmes, you sent her."

"I did no such thing."

"Then how could you possibly know all those details."

"Mrs. Hudson told me," he laughed. "Sometimes the simplest explanation is the true one."

"But you've only just returned home. I heard the front door open and you ascending the stairs immediately after. You didn't have time to speak to her."

"Watson, you miss the obvious."

"Do I?" I asked, rather annoyed with my friend.

"I came in, just as I left this morning, through the rear door. You know Mrs. Hudson prefers I use the tradesmen's entrance when I am attired like this. She then told me everything that had transpired. It only required my opening and closing the front door rather loudly to create the illusion that I had just arrived home."

I had to laugh in spite of myself because as Holmes had so often admonished me, I had jumped to a conclusion without considering any other possibilities. "Well, what do you make of Mrs. Werth's visit?"

"Why was she here?"

Seeing a chance to return the favor, I asked innocently, "Why don't you ask Mrs. Hudson?"

"Very good, Watson. However, I am afraid only you can provide me with that information."

"She said she was newly married, that her husband had suddenly changed on their wedding night, and she now feared for her life."

"An excellent summary. Wonderfully concise and devoid of so many of the lurid details which so often find their way into your accounts of our adventures. Did she say where she was from?"

"Yes, I believe she mentioned Shrewsbury in Shropshire."

"Was Werth her maiden name or her married name?"

"I never thought to ask. But I feel that we must do something to assist her."

Holmes sighed, "And so we shall." With that, he sat and composed a telegram. He then rang for the buttons and instructed the lad to send the telegram he had just written and to wait for a response. "It may take some time, so treat yourself to cake and tea while you wait." With that he reached into his pocket and handed the lad some coins.

The youngster then clattered down the stairs and slammed the front door as he left.

"What was that all about?"

"I am testing a theory," he replied. "Shrewsbury in Shropshire is not an overly large village. I have simply made a rather discreet inquiry to see if members of the local constabulary, the West Mercian police, are familiar with your Miss Werth and to inquire about any weddings which may have occurred there within the past two weeks.

"By the way, Watson, did you happen to notice her wedding ring?"

I was sorely tempted to lie and say that she had worn gloves, but I knew Holmes would see right through me. "I must confess..."

Cutting me off, Holmes said, "No matter, we shall know more in a bit. Now let me wash and change my attire before supper."

Over our meal, I asked my friend how his day had gone. "Not as well as I might have hoped. I am trying to ascertain who owns the warehouse the smugglers were using, but, for some reason, that is proving far more difficult than it should. Truth be told, Watson, I am sensing a greater force at work here than we might have at first imagined."

"Why do you say that?"

"Consider, I can sometimes go two weeks without a case, and suddenly we have three – if you include Mycroft's request – all of which clamor for our full attention. And this latest one – your Mrs. Werth – would make four, and it would appear to require us to leave London and travel to the Midlands in order to bring about a solution. It all seems a bit …"

"Overwhelming?" I suggested.

"I was thinking more along the lines of staged," he replied. "But to what end?" my friend continued.

"If I may be so bold …"

"Reticence? Now? It hardly suits you," laughed Holmes. "Come, out with it, Watson."

"These other cases, while they are certainly important in their own right, pale beside the importance of the request made by your brother."

"I agree. While I was on the docks, I looked for signs of anything unusual and discovered nothing. I also received no reports of any strange occurrences from the Irregulars. What makes it so confounding is that I have only the vaguest idea of what I am seeking. It's not as if a ship were to dock, and the crew members announce themselves as here to disrupt the peace conference as they disembark. And yet, I cannot shake the feeling that there are strings being pulled. There is a certain pattern that seems to be emerging, but at this point, it is impossible to discern exactly what the configuration might be."

"For now we see through a glass, darkly; but then face to face: now I know in part; but then shall I know even as also I am known," I said.

"A quote from the New Testament! And an apropos one. Bravo, Watson! I would counter that for things to become clearer, I am going to have to look through my glass starkly," he said, holding up his lens with a flourish. Although he had changed the meaning of glass entirely, I was still impressed by the nimbleness of wit my friend constantly exhibited.

We continued our discussion over cigarettes and port, when a soft knock at the door interrupted our conversation.

"Come in," said Holmes.

At that point, the buttons entered the room, "I waited as you instructed, Mr. Holmes. Here is the reply," he said handing my friend an envelope.

Holmes gave the lad a few more coppers. After the youngster had departed, he opened the envelope. After reading the contents over twice, he laughed and handed me the telegram, saying as he did so, "The pattern has just become a little bit clearer, I think."

Taking the envelope from Holmes, I read:

NO FAMILY NAMED WERTH KNOWN IN SHREWSBURY. STOP. NO WEDDINGS HERE IN LAST TWO WEEKS. STOP. SGT. MCELROY.

Chapter 8

"What does it mean, Holmes?"

"It means things are not always what they seem. It would also imply that in some subtle way we are being manipulated."

"What is our next move then?"

"I believe we are best served by feigning ignorance and thus allowing the puppet master to continue to think he is pulling the strings unobserved. We have just had a glimpse into his plans. As you suggested, these 'cases' are all deliberate attempts to distract us."

"But from what? And to what end?"

"That remains to be seen," replied my friend. "Although I must say, I have my suspicions."

No matter how hard I pressed the issue, Holmes refused to enlighten me. Turning to another oft-repeated phrase, he said, "You have seen what I have seen. You know what I know. Now, put yourself in my shoes and see if you can't sort out this tangled skein."

Over the next two days, I saw little of Holmes. He would rise early, breakfast alone and quit our lodgings before I had even awakened. A few clients stopped by looking for him, but when they found out he was unavailable, they would either leave a card or write their name and address on a piece of paper. Rather than seeing one disappointed face after another, I tried to ease their anxiety by informing them Holmes was out of the country, and it was impossible to say when he might return.

In a few cases, that little white lie seemed to allay their fears, and I didn't think Holmes would mind.

I was quite surprised when late one night, I heard Holmes bound up the stairs. He entered looking quite pleased with himself. Before I could say anything, he smiled at me. "If you are going to tell people that I am out of the country, I think we would be better served if you offered them something concrete. You might tell them I was summoned to Rome by the Pope, or I had to journey to America at the behest of the Rockefellers. Specifics are always far more believable than vague generalities."

"So you would turn my little lie into a far more grand deception?"

"Little lies, big lies. Come, Watson, let's not mince words: An untruth is an untruth."

"We can discuss the finer points of mendacity later. In the meantime, have you made any progress?"

At my words, Holmes went to the window and gazed down on Baker Street. He then opened the door and looked in the hall. After another glance out the window, he turned to me and said, "It is as I suspected. There is a common thread linking the theft of the *Beowulf* manuscript, Lestrade's smuggling ring and the upcoming peace conference and quite possibly the mysterious Miss Werth."

"My word!" I exclaimed. "Who is behind these things?"

"That has yet to be determined. But whoever he is, he apparently looks upon me as a threat and so he has engineered all these attempts to distract me and occupy my time."

"How did you discover the link?"

"It was a most singular revelation," explained Holmes. "I was walking by the Marble Arch, doing a bit of reconnoitering and considering the best way to disrupt a peace conference in a formidable building that is not only a national treasure but which also houses a police station."

"And what did you conclude?"

"Any such attack would have to be a multi-pronged one, and as I imagined various scenarios, it hit me at that moment that I was the one under siege."

"That's all well and good," I explained. "And I am glad to see you are finally giving Mycroft's request the attention it deserves, but the fact remains that you still have two other cases to solve."

"Indeed," my friend replied, "but now I can look at them properly. I can re-evaluate them from an entirely different perspective, and I am hopeful this new-found vantage point will yield results sooner rather than later."

"How did you arrive at this rather startling conclusion?"

"Criminals are creatures of habit, Watson. The smugglers learn the police are coming: What do they do?"

"Why, they escape, lay low for a bit and then open in a new location."

Holmes peered at me curiously then he said, "Watson, you are getting quite good at this game; I do hope you never develop any criminal tendencies. At any rate, you are quite right, but the truth is the smugglers appear to have vanished entirely. The restaurants they were serving have returned to their old vendors and are once again paying full price. In fact, no one has heard from the smugglers since shortly before the raid."

"So you mean the whole thing was , . ."

"A sham," exclaimed Holmes, "designed to do exactly what it did. Truth be told, I would not be surprised to learn that the whole smuggling operation was little more than an elaborate charade. They may have even paid full price for the brandies and wines and then sold them at a loss to foster the illusion."

"What a piece of deviltry! But will you be able to help Lestrade?"

"I have spoken to the Inspector and explained that it may take some time as his case is inextricably linked with two others."

"And how did he react?"

"As you might expect. He is champing at the bit to return to work, but I also think he is enjoying the time off. After all, he isn't too far from retirement, so this enforced leave is serving as a sort of precursor."

"I hadn't thought of that," I confessed.

"As he admitted to me in a rare moment of candor, 'There is more to life than police work, Mr. Holmes.'"

After he had filled his pipe, Holmes turned to me and said, "So now, we must chart a new course, one that focuses on the peace conference, which is probably now just two weeks away."

"And what of Dr. Smith? And *Cotton Vitellius A XV*?"

"All part of the same problem. Once we are able to solve one aspect of this case, I am certain the others will fall neatly into place."

"And where will you begin?"

"At the beginning, of course," replied Holmes.

Although I knew Holmes was waiting for me to ask, since I had a pretty good idea of where this whole thing had originated, I held my tongue.

After a rather lengthy silence, Holmes laughed, "I cannot believe you would deny me my little bit of psychic legerdemain." He then continued, "You may recall that Mycroft admitted that someone in the government 'let the cat out of the bag' as he put it about my presence in Paris. Given everything that has transpired and the enormous stakes, I am now rather inclined to think the bag was deliberately opened and the cat released on purpose."

"You don't mean a spy in Mycroft's office?"

"What other explanation could there possibly be? At any rate, such a theory ties everything neatly together. I was nearly waylaid because somehow, my presence in Paris was revealed. Then after escaping from the ruffians in France, I suddenly find myself deluged with all manner of cases. No Watson, the puppet master is real. When we discover who is behind the curtain, pulling the strings, I am certain that everything will become crystal clear, including the relationship between such seemingly disparate events."

"So what will you do?"

"I have a plan. Right now, it is but a rough idea. However, I shall refine it and perfect it so that when it is finished, I may say: 'He has dug a hole and hollowed it out; he has fallen into the pit of his making.'"

I cannot say which surprised me more: Holmes' revelation that there was a spy in the upper echelons of the government or the fact that after teasing me recently, he was now quoting from the Bible himself.

Looking at him, I could only guess, "Proverbs?"

"No," replied my friend, "Psalms. Now, a bit more brandy?"

The next morning Holmes was gone when I awoke, so I ate alone. He returned midway through the meal and joined me.

"You're up early," I said.

"I had some pieces to put into place before our visit with Mycroft."

"I didn't know we were visiting your brother."

"Neither does he," replied Holmes and then he deftly changed the subject.

Later that day, Holmes and I paid that unannounced call on Mycroft at his office. Although his secretary informed us that Mycroft was in a meeting and could not possibly be disturbed, Holmes barged right by him, as I trailed behind, insisting loudly, as I had been instructed to do, that the information we had for his brother was of paramount importance and that Mycroft must be made aware of it immediately.

A moment later, we entered Mycroft's office. He and four members of his staff had been sitting at a large table off to the side of Mycroft's desk. On the table had been spread a detailed map of some sort. Mycroft started to rise, but Holmes rushed to the table, gesturing for his brother to remain seated.

"Sherlock, I do hope this is important. I am meeting with my top aides regarding progress in The Hague and our upcoming conference."

Bowing to those at the table, Holmes said, "Gentlemen, my sincerest apologies for the disturbance. However, my brother had asked me to contact him immediately were I to learn of anything untoward." Gesturing for me to join him, Holmes introduced me, saying, "This is my friend and colleague, Dr. John Watson."

All four stood up to shake my hand, and the first one introduced himself as Geoffrey Langlois, who informed me his area of expertise was France. He was quite tall with a short, neatly trimmed dark beard that was just showing the first traces of gray. I noted that his suit was of the finest wool and he seemed confident and self-assured. After he had finished, he sat down and continued reading the papers before him.

The second young man said, "I am Diedrich Bern, and as you might guess, I focus on developments within Germany and Austria." Although Bern was small and slight, he looked as though he were quite athletic. He seemed a bit more reserved than Langlois.

The third young man, who was very slender and seemed almost timid by comparison to the first two, extended his hand, and said in a soft voice, "Alexander Dennison, I do my best to keep up with events in Mother Russia."

Finally, the last of the group shook my hand, informing me, "I am Deniz Cenk, and my area of expertise is the Ottoman Empire." He seemed a number of years older than the others, and his attire was not nearly as fine as theirs.

Clearing his throat, Mycroft brought the room to silence. Looking at Holmes, he said, "We are quite busy, but you said you had urgent news."

"I do," replied Holmes, "regarding the Tenrev Brigade." With that, my friend reached into his pocket and withdrew an envelope, which he passed to his brother. "I think you will find this of considerable interest, and I trust that you will know how to employ it." Turning back to the table, Holmes said, "We have taken up enough of your precious time, and I am certain that you have important matters to consider. Gentlemen, Mycroft, I bid you good day."

After we had left Mycroft's office, I started to question Holmes, but with an almost imperceptible shake of his head, he bade me be silent. After we had reached the street, he pulled his pipe from his pocket and tapped the bowl four times, knocking out the few bits of remaining ash, even though I had not seen him smoke all morning. Since he did not light the pipe, I thought it rather odd, but said nothing about it.

I continued to honor his wishes, and it was only when we were safely ensconced in a hansom on our way to Baker Street that Holmes began to chuckle. Looking at me, he said, "Well done, Watson. You have been the long-suffering servant in this little charade, and I thank you for your indulgence."

"Charade?" I asked incredulously. "Holmes, I thought we were trying to prevent a cataclysm, and now you describe our work as a farce."

"Watson, I say charade, but perhaps deception might be a more apt description. I have scattered the first few breadcrumbs on the path. Now we must wait to see who, if anyone, attempts to follow the trail."

"You believe the spy is someone in Mycroft's office?"

"I do not know for certain, but I must start somewhere."

"Did you learn anything else?"

"Quite a bit, actually," replied my friend. "Although I am not certain that any of it is relevant to the matter at hand."

"And what were the breadcrumbs that you tossed?"

"If you recall, I mentioned the 'Tenrev Brigade' to Mycroft.'

"Yes. What is it? I have never heard of it."

"Truth be told, there is no Tenrev Brigade," explained Holmes. "Actually, Tenrev is simply Vernet spelled backwards. I am certain Mycroft will see the connection immediately."

I realized that Holmes had merely reversed the letters of his grandmother's maiden name to create his fictitious faction. "And now we wait to see which of Mycroft's aides seeks more information about this group?"

"Bravo, Watson," said Holmes. "I feel certain we will make a detective of you yet."

Since I was a bit nettled at myself for failing to see through Holmes' rather simple pretext, I decided to take his comment in stride.

After making a few stops for tobacco and other sundries, we returned to Baker Street to discover a nattily attired young lad waiting for us in the sitting room.

He rose when we entered, extended his hand and said simply, "I am Alastair. Your brother gave me this note and instructed me to wait until I had delivered it to you in person."

"Well, you have accomplished your mission," said Holmes.

"Then I'll be on my way," replied the youth.

Holmes attempted to give the lad a few coins, but the youngster replied, "While I appreciate the gesture, sir, Mister Mycroft would have my head." With that, he bowed and left.

Holmes then opened the note, read it over twice and chuckled.

"Something amusing?" I asked.

"Mycroft has had the foresight to make the Tenrev Brigade active among the docks." The look on my face must have betrayed me, for Holmes added, "Don't you see? By assigning the faction's base of operations to the waterfront, my brother is also allowing me to pursue my attempts to clear Lestrade at the same time."

"Do you think he did it deliberately?"

"With Mycroft, every move is carefully considered. In his own subtle way, my brother is also trying to help the Inspector, so the least we can do is accommodate his wishes."

"When you say 'we,' am I to take it that you are using that in a figurative sense?"

"Not at all, Watson. The docks spread out for miles on both sides of the Thames. While this would normally be a job for a brigade of men, we do have the Irregulars assisting us."

"As you just pointed out, there are miles of docks. They stretch from Woolwich to the Tower on both sides of the river and that's not even taking into account the newer docks downstream."

"Yes, but I think we can start by focusing on the Royal Victoria Docks and the Royal Albert Dock and possibly the Graving Docks on the other side of the Thames. The warehouse that served as the smugglers' base of operations is located right near the canal connecting the Albert and Victoria docks, so that seems like the logical place to begin."

"Must we go in disguise?"

Holmes chuckled and pointed his pipe stem at me, "If we don't, I am dreadfully afraid that we will look somewhat out of place."

"Just this once, couldn't we pose as tea merchants or tobacco importers instead of laborers?"

"Watson, a matelot can go anywhere. A tea or tobacco merchant or any type of trader is confined to those docks that carry his product."

Although it pained me to admit it, Holmes was correct in his assessment of the situation. Seeing my obvious displeasure, he said warmly, "Cheer up. I will treat you to dinner, and you may choose the restaurant."

Seeing an opportunity to make my friend atone – at least in a financial way – for the hardships to be visited upon me in the near future, I decided to dine at the Criterion.

As we sat there that evening, I recalled how a chance encounter with Stamford in this very establishment many years earlier had led to my being introduced to Sherlock Holmes. As I reflected on our years together and the many cases in which we had been involved, Holmes suddenly interrupted my thoughts, proclaiming, "It has been a long, strange journey, indeed."

I smiled at my companion and replied only, "Indeed."

Early the next morning, I was roused from my bed by a thoroughly disreputably dressed Holmes, who proclaimed, "Time and tide wait for no man, Watson." Handing me a pile of clothes, he said, "Put these on, and we will talk over breakfast."

After dressing, I joined my friend for a rather rushed meal of coffee, toast and eggs. "So what is the plan?" I asked.

"Today, I want to examine the warehouse where the smugglers allegedly operated. Since I do not have permission to enter the premises, I will need you to serve as my lookout. You must be sharp at all times, and if anything should strike you as unusual, please inform me at once."

Despite the early hour and our appearance, we were able to hire a cab to take us to Stansfeld Road. Holmes had the driver stop about a mile from the river, and we then walked to the docks.

Long before we arrived at the circular junction that joined Dockside Road with the Royal Albert Dock, we could see lorries and other vehicles transporting various goods into the City of London. When we finally arrived at the river, it was a veritable beehive of activity. Spotting a hand-truck sitting idle against the side of a building, Holmes "borrowed" it, saying, "This will give you something to do."

As we walked along, we could smell the river and hear the cacophony of men bellowing orders, horses neighing, and laborers complaining. Twice during our trek we heard the triple blast of a ship's horn signaling its arrival and drowning out all the other noise. After some half-hour, we arrived at a warehouse that seemed deserted compared to its counterparts.

Holmes and I lounged against the wall and lit cigarettes. After a few minutes, he said to me, "I am going to try to find another entrance. If you think anyone is about to enter the warehouse while I am inside, bang on the front door as loudly as you can and yell, 'I know you are in there Mr. Margate.'"

Perhaps another thirty minutes had passed before Holmes reappeared, during which time I was twice offered work. Hoisting a box on his shoulder, Holmes said, "Follow me, Watson."

We proceeded back the way we had come perhaps an hour before. When we had finally reached Stansfeld Road, Holmes said, "I do believe that was time well spent."

"What on Earth could you have discovered that the police missed?"

"They didn't miss anything, Watson. They police saw the clues; in fact, they were quite difficult to miss. But, as usual, they failed to appreciate the significance of what was sitting right in front of them."

"And what is it that they overlooked?"

"The safe and the desk, Watson! Both pieces were high quality, and they didn't simply materialize in that warehouse. In fact, when you consider that both items played crucial roles in establishing Lestrade's alleged guilt, one can only wonder why the police didn't think to examine them more closely.

"The safe in that office was manufactured by Chubb and Son, and it is one of their newest fire-resistant models. Someone obviously went to a great deal of trouble to install a very expensive safe in that warehouse. As to why, well on that point I can only speculate. Still, a visit to the Chubb factory on Glengall Road off Old Kent Road, may help us discover the name of the buyer. If that happens, we will have taken a very large step forward in our efforts to clear Lestrade.

"If that should prove fruitless, we can then visit the Lebus factory in Tottenham. With its secret drawer, that desk was obviously custom-made, plus it was constructed of walnut rather than oak. Even though they produce thousands of pieces a year, I am certain that desk will stick in someone's memory.

"Now, let us return to Baker Street, adjust our appearance and prepare to visit the Chubb factory."

"But don't you want to check on the rest of the docks?"

"That's all being taken care of, old friend," Holmes said. He then lapsed into silence as we walked up Stansfeld Road and finally found a cab willing to take us home. I was excited at the prospect of possibly clearing Lestrade, and I was even more overjoyed at the idea of doffing my disguise and enjoying a proper wash. Looking at Holmes, with his chin buried in his chest, I decided to let sleeping detectives lie. I knew he would tell me about the docks when he was ready.

Chapter 9

After we had returned home, Holmes quickly dispatched several wires and then we both enjoyed a lunch of cold roast beef and horseradish sauce, I felt refreshed and reinvigorated. After we had eaten, Holmes received two replies to his earlier communiqués, and so we hailed a cab and headed back across the river over the Westminster Bridge. We then followed Westminster Bridge Road to Old Kent Road and then to Glengall Road. We were now in an industrial area, home to any number of factories, and when we arrived at the premises of Chubb and Son, Holmes instructed the driver to wait.

During the ride, Holmes had told me something of the background of the Chubb family. According to my friend, the business, now in its third generation, had been founded by Charles Chubb, who passed it to his son, John Chubb. He, in turn, had left the business to his sons. However, in 1882, the business had been purchased from the trustees and formed into a limited company under the chairmanship of George Hayter Chubb, while his brothers, John Charles and Harry Withers, served as directors.

The family had risen to fame with the invention of the famed detector lock nearly a century ago. The lock had defied all attempts to pick it for more than thirty years. It finally yielded to the machinations of Alfred Hobbs, an American locksmith and inventor, at the Great Exposition in 1851. Following its conquest, the Chubb family immediately set about making their locks even more secure.

"I have had some experience with Chubb locks over the years as you may recall, Watson, and as a result I have become acquainted with John Charles Chubb. I wired him earlier, and he has agreed to meet with us this afternoon."

Upon entering the building, we found ourselves in a large room with hundreds of workers. Some were crafting locks while others were assembling safes. The din was almost unbearable. One of the workers led us to the back, and we were shown into John Charles Chubb's private office. No sooner had he closed the door then the noise ceased. To say I was equal parts amazed and relieved would be to capture my mood perfectly.

"Mr. Holmes," said Chubb, rising from behind his desk, "it is a pleasure to see you again."

"And you, Mr. Chubb," said Holmes. Turning to me, Holmes said, "I would like to introduce my friend and colleague, Dr. John Watson."

Shaking my hand warmly, Chubb said, "It is a pleasure to meet you at long last, Dr. Watson. I do so enjoy your stories in *The Strand*. And I must say every time you mention a Chubb lock, we see a definite uptick in business."

Turning to Holmes, he said, "Have you a question about locks, Mr. Holmes?"

"Actually, no," replied Holmes, "I do, however, have a question about safes."

Holmes then described the safe he had seen in the warehouse in great detail and asked Chubb if he knew how many they had sold recently.

"From your description, it sounds like one of our newer models. Just bear with me a second," he asked as he opened the top drawer in a file cabinet. Pulling a sheet of paper from a folder, he gazed at it and then asked Holmes, "You said it was approximately 18 inches wide and 24 inches high?"

"I did," said Holmes.

"And the nameplate simply said, 'Chubb' with 'Patent Safe' beneath it? There was no business name inscribed below that?"

After rifling through a few more file folders, Chubb turned to us and said, "I have it right here. Now that I see the bill of sale, I remember it well because we almost always emboss the name of the business on the plate under our own. It is quite a rare thing when we don't."

"So then you know who purchased it," I asked excitedly.

"Of course, it was ordered by one M. Holmes, and he asked that we deliver it to a warehouse on the Royal Albert Docks," said Chubb. "Is he any relation?"

"I do have a brother named Mycroft," said my friend, "but I can assure you he did not purchase the safe. I am sorry to have taken up your time. However, I do have one more question?"

"By all means," said Chubb.

"When was the safe ordered?"

"On the 6th of December of last year," replied Chubb.

After we had escaped the pandemonium of the factory, I said to Holmes, "Well that was a bit of a wild goose chase."

"Not entirely," he replied. He then instructed our driver to take us to Tottenham. During the rather lengthy ride, Holmes related the story of Louis Lebus, who had emigrated from Germany perhaps 80 years ago and started a small business which had become wildly successful. His son, Harris, now ran the business and had recently moved the firm from the East End to Tottenham, so he could erect a larger factory. "I am told he now employs more than 1,000 workers," said Holmes and with that he lapsed into silence.

When we arrived in Tottenham, I was taken aback by the sheer size of the factory. Having roused himself, Holmes explained that when purchasing the land, Lebus had chosen a spot near a dock on the river Lea. I also noticed that it was located right next to a railroad line.

After presenting his card, we were shown into the office of Harris Lebus. It was a handsome room, with furniture that had obviously been expressly crafted to his specifications.

"Mr. Holmes, what a pleasure finally to meet you," said Lebus, shaking my friend's hand. Turning to me and grasping my hand, he said, "And I assume that you must be Dr. Watson. I am delighted, gentlemen. How may I be of assistance?"

"I wonder if I might ask you a few questions about a desk which I believe you produced," said Holmes.

"I shall endeavor to help, but we produce so many desks every year, thousands in fact. Is there something special about this particular desk?"

"Actually, there are two things," replied Holmes. "To start with, it is made of walnut."

"Well, that does rather narrow things considerably," replied Lebus. "Most of our desks are constructed of oak. A walnut desk would be a special order and it would be hand-crafted. But you said there are two things, Mr. Holmes."

"Indeed, this particular desk had a secret compartment constructed behind the lower drawer on the right-hand side."

I thought I detected a flicker of recognition pass across Lebus' face. "I believe I remember the exact piece," he said. "The secret compartment entailed quite a bit of extra work, so we had to charge significantly more than we usually do for that type of desk."

As he was speaking, he moved to an ornate file cabinet and pulling open the third drawer from the top, he began rifling through papers. Pulling one out, he exclaimed, "Here it is, the bill of sale."

He handed it to Holmes, who examined it and then began to chuckle. Passing the paper to me, I examined it and saw that the desk had been ordered by one "G. Lestrade" the previous December.

As we were leaving the factory, Holmes said, "He taunts me, Watson, but I assure you, I will have the last laugh."

After we had reached the street, and there were no cabs to be found, Holmes suggested we take the train back to London. As we walked to the nearby Tottenham

Hale station, he said, "I believe it will be faster by train, if we can time things correctly."

"Of course," I said. "I just can't believe that we have followed the clues to this rascal from pillar to post and have nothing to show for it."

At that Holmes stopped walking, looked at me and said, "I will meet you at the station." With that, he turned and began walking briskly back to the factory.

I made my way to the station where I waited patiently for Holmes. One London-bound train passed as I kept my lonely vigil, and it was only ten minutes before the next one was due to arrive when Holmes appeared on the platform.

"Well?" I inquired.

"Let us just say that was time well spent. I believe we have taken another step forward to clearing Lestrade as well as to tying up all those other loose ends."

"Does that include the missing *Cotton Vitellius A XV*?"

"What about it?"

"You have been tasked with recovering it."

"Watson, I am certain the manuscript to be in a very safe place. For now, it must appear as though we have made no progress in that direction. The *Nowell Codex* may yet play a significant role in this case, but if we were to return it to Dr. Smith, we will have removed that piece from the board, something I am loath to do."

I could not believe my ears. I was stunned by the fact that Holmes believed he had located the *Codex*, but I was even more upset that he had kept the knowledge to himself.

"I am disappointed in you, Holmes."

"Watson, you wear your heart on your sleeve, and your inability to mask your emotions, while it may be endearing to some – especially those of the opposite sex – can prove quite a hindrance to someone in my line of work. I ask your forgiveness and your indulgence. I do not enjoy keeping you in the dark, but there are times when I do it out of concern for your safety."

Given Holmes usual reticence about such matters, I found it easy to forgive him and I said so.

"After all," he said, "it was merely a sin of omission, and now that has been rectified."

At that moment, we both heard the whistle of a steam engine as it approached the station. During the rather brief ride to the Liverpool Street Station, Holmes partially explained his train of thought regarding the disappearance of the *Beowulf* manuscript. When he had finished, I said, "Well, that seems all well and good, but you still have a few loose ends to tie together."

"Watson, I assure you they will fall into place. Now, tomorrow, I have several things to which I must attend in the morning, and then in the afternoon I mean to pay another visit to the Marble Arch. Would you care to accompany me?"

"I certainly would. I know you feel as though you have everything under control, but I am still worried about this peace conference. There are fewer than two weeks remaining before it is scheduled to convene, and as yet you have not discovered any sort of threat."

"Given what transpired in Paris, I must admit I am somewhat surprised we have failed to ascertain any activity. I would have thought between the Irregulars and my other informants that we might have caught wind of something by now, but the silence is deafening."

"So what will you do?"

"I will continue to remain vigilant and try to prepare for any and all eventualities."

Saying that, Holmes lapsed into silence and remained reticent for the remainder of the ride home and all through dinner. Later, he pulled out several of his indexes, and I decided that any attempts at conversation would be rebuffed, so I read for a bit and then turned in. As I lie in bed, I realized what a long day it had been and was soon asleep.

I awoke the next morning shortly after nine. Feeling refreshed, I dressed but I soon discovered that Holmes had once again eaten and departed the premises perhaps an hour before. Uncertain of when he would return, I decided to remain at Baker Street as he had asked me to accompany him to the Marble Arch in the afternoon.

I was surprised when I heard his familiar tread on the stairs at just after 11. When he entered, he seemed in a fairly upbeat mood. "I gather your morning went well."

"Indeed," said Holmes, "I think that we are quite close to clearing Lestrade, and I have also reassured Dr. Smith about the safety of the *Beowulf* manuscript."

"But you are not going to act on either of those?"

"No, Watson. To act now would be to reveal that we have tumbled to the plan to distract and waylay us. Rather, we must be seen to be looking into both cases with the assiduousness that characterizes all my investigations, if one were to believe your rather florid prose."

I laughed in spite of myself because I was genuinely pleased to see that Holmes had made progress, and could now focus on the peace conference which was drawing nigh rapidly. If Mycroft adhered to his original timetable, we had only another ten or eleven days before it would begin.

"Are we still visiting the Marble Arch?"

"Indeed," he replied, "directly after lunch. And then I may have a very important task that I would like you to carry out for me."

"As always, Holmes, I am at your service."

After our meal, we decided, since the weather was quite lovely following a morning shower, to walk to the Marble Arch. As we strolled along Baker Street to George Street and then to Great Cumberland Street, Holmes explained that he thought Mycroft's choice of the Arch for the peace conference was inspired.

"Consider," he said, "we have a cast off piece of Buckingham Palace that now houses a police station. Mycroft has hidden his secret meeting right out in the open."

When we finally arrived, I wondered how the foreign dignitaries would react to this now rather dingy looking monument to excess that had been shunted off to the side like some out-of-favor relative.

Originally designed by John Nash in 1827 to be the state entrance to the *cour d'honneur* of Buckingham Palace, the Marble Arch had been modeled on the Arch of Constantine in Rome and the Arc de Triomphe in Paris. Its creator had envisioned a tribute to England's victories at Trafalgar and Waterloo. However, following the death of King George IV, his successor, William IV, wanted nothing to do with Buckingham and had tried to convince Parliament to settle there. With the ascension of Queen Victoria to the throne, Buckingham Palace had been enlarged and expanded to accommodate her growing family, and the Arch had been moved to make room for the renovations.

In 1851, the Arch was disassembled and moved stone by stone to its present location where it served as a grand entrance to Hyde Park and the Great Exposition of that year.

Although it may appear solid to the casual passerby, there are actually three small rooms inside the arch, capable of housing a dozen officers and a sergeant. Once you are inside, it is like being in a fortress, and I too began to see the genius of Mycroft's plan. As we strolled around the grimy marble, I couldn't help but wonder how it might have looked when it was first completed decades ago and its color had been a pristine white.

"Yes, I think my brother has chosen well," remarked Holmes. "The structure appears impregnable. Several guards will be at hand; moreover, their presence will attract no undue attention. It is also possible the inevitable crowd of sightseers may function as another, subtle layer of protection."

"Does that mean the conference is secure?"

"Not at all, Watson. It simply means that any attempt to disrupt the meetings will not take place here. So we must ask Mycroft where the delegates are staying when they arrive."

"Wouldn't they reside at their respective embassies?"

"I should hardly think so, Watson. Remember, this is a secret peace conference, and I am certain there are all types of watchers from any number of countries keeping an eye on both the French and Russian embassies. No, if I know Mycroft, he will book rooms for them in two different hotels."

"Why different hotels?"

"The last thing Mycroft needs is some sort of deal brokered behind his back between his two alleged 'allies.' No I rather think they will be kept far apart for as much of their stay here as is possible.

"I rather suspect that he will book rooms for the Russians at Brown's Hotel, which is less than two miles from here, while ensconcing the French at the Savoy, which is considerably further away. I am certain he will make every attempt to ensure their paths never cross.

Neutrality will most certainly rule the day – at least if Mycroft has any say in the matter."

"Well, it sounds as though you have been giving this a great deal of consideration."

"Indeed, I have," replied Holmes. "Despite your remonstrations, the conference has never been far from my thoughts – even as I labored on the other cases."

"Where to now?" I asked.

"I think back to Baker Street. I am anxiously awaiting word from Wiggins."

"What has Wiggins to do with this?"

"Ever since I planted the notion of the Tenrev Brigade, I have had the Irregulars following each of Mycroft's assistants."

"So, you suspect one of them of being the spy?"

"While Mycroft is secretive to a fault, he is usually an excellent judge of character. However, I think it quite likely that an accomplished spy, one most likely installed here years ago, perhaps even decades, may have been able to succeed in securing himself some sort of mid-level position within the government and then working his way up through the ranks. Given the right gifts and provided with the proper contacts, such a man could hardly fail to attract the attention of my brother, who is always seeking out the best and the brightest young minds."

"But if Mycroft is the British government, what need has he of these assistants?"

"As you have noted, Watson, my brother is sedentary to a fault. When lower-level meetings are held, he generally dispatches one of his minions in his place. They report back to him, and he then analyzes the information and determines how best to use it to England's advantage.

"We know each of the four men has a degree of expertise in the affairs of a particular country. If travel is required, for any sort of conference, Mycroft merely chooses the proper assistant, provides him with very specific instructions and sends him out in the name of 'King and Country.'"

Saying that, Holmes turned on his heel and hailed a cab to take us back to our lodgings. Little did we suspect that this day which had begun so innocuously would end on a decidedly different note.

Chapter 10

As we alighted from the cab, I spotted Wiggins leaning casually on the lamppost across the street. I was about to wave to him when Holmes grabbed my arm, and pushed me back into the cab. "Go to your club," he said quietly, "and remain there until midnight unless you have heard from me before then."

As you might expect, I was slightly miffed and more than a little bewildered, but the tone of Holmes voice told me that he would brook no argument on this point.

I arrived at the club around five and spent an hour reading the papers. At that point, I decided to order dinner. After a solitary meal, I retired to the billiard room. Although it was not our usual night, Thurston arrived and by nine o'clock, I had won back all the money and then some that I had lost the previous week.

After he departed, I was wondering how I might pass the time until midnight when a note arrived from Holmes informing me that it was safe to return to Baker Street.

When I arrived at Baker Street, I found Holmes sitting in his chair, smoking his old cherrywood pipe, deep in thought. "Pray tell, Holmes, what was all that about this afternoon?" I asked.

"You saw Wiggins lounging across the street when we arrived?"

"Indeed, I did."

"The fact that he was leaning against the left side of the lamppost, as viewed from our front door, was a prearranged signal to me that our lodgings were under surveillance. Had he stationed himself on the right side, it would have signaled that all was well."

"My word."

"I sent you to your club for safekeeping ..."

"Safekeeping!" I exclaimed angrily. "Holmes, I am not some child who must be watched over."

"Watson, these are dangerous men."

"Yes, and we have faced many such adversaries in the past, and we have generally faced them *together*."

"And so we shall again, my friend."

"Not if you have decided that I must be bundled off for safekeeping. Need I remind you of the night we captured Colonel Moran or the vigil we held waiting for John Clay to break into the bank vault?"

I believe that Holmes could see how angry and hurt I was. He looked at me, paused and then said, "It will not happen again, I promise you."

I nodded. "So tell me what transpired after I left for my club."

"I walked from Baker Street over to Paddington where I keep a bolt hole. I quickly disguised myself as a Roman Catholic priest, but when I emerged from my hidey-hole, Wiggins was nowhere to be seen.

"Wiggins arrived here about an hour ago. He said the man he had under surveillance had followed me to Paddington and noted the building I had entered. Wiggins thinks the man might have might have spotted him, for the man headed for the Underground, and despite Wiggins' best efforts, he lost him in a crowd.

"As I said, when I emerged from the building, Wiggins was nowhere in sight. After making certain I was no longer being followed, I doffed my disguise, returned here and sent for you."

"What does it mean, Holmes?"

"Unless I miss my guess, we are starting to make someone nervous, and I think that bodes well for the future. However, it also means that we must never let our guard down."

Before he could continue, we heard the bell ring, and a moment later, Mrs. Hudson knocked on the door.

"Come in, Mrs. Hudson," said Holmes.

Our landlady entered carrying an envelope. "This just arrived by messenger, Mr. Holmes. I was instructed to deliver it to you as soon as possible."

Rising, Holmes walked to the door, took the envelope from our landlady, thanked her and escorted her out. Closing the door behind her, he tore open the envelope and after reading the note, announced, "Mycroft would like to see us at the Diogenes Club as soon as possible."

Outside, we hailed a cab and a short while later, we were sitting in the Stranger's Room, waiting for Mycroft. He entered a few minutes later and after settling his considerable bulk into the wing chair that he favored, asked, "So what, if any, progress have you made?" Without waiting for an answer, he continued, "You simply must do better. Due to unforeseen circumstances, I have had to move the conference up, and it is now scheduled to get under way in just four days' time."

Although the news surprised my friend, he retained his equanimity and merely said, "That certainly changes things a bit." Holmes then related the events of the day, including the fact that our lodgings now appeared to be under surveillance.

"Yes, I am inclined to think that your Tenrev Brigade has proven to be a rather effective gambit. However, it pains me to think that one of my trusted aides might well be a spy. To that end, I am now consulting with each man separately, rather than at general staff meetings, in an effort to limit any further damage. I have also instructed each man to keep our conversations confidential."

"I should think one carefully placed false report might be enough to ferret out the informant," said Holmes.

"Normally, I would agree, but these are four very bright young men. Anything that might be used to deceive them is going to have to be terribly convincing."

"And so it shall," exclaimed Holmes.

"What do you have in mind?" asked Mycroft.

Holmes then outlined a plan that can only be described as equal parts brilliance and audacity.

When he had finished, Mycroft looked at him and said, "I have never fully appreciated the depths of your deviousness until now."

"So you agree?" asked my friend.

"Let me consider it, as well as all the possible ramifications, and I will give you an answer tomorrow evening. Shall we say at seven?"

"Excellent," replied Holmes. "I just hope we are acting in time."

On the way home in the cab, I said to Holmes, "Do you think this plan of yours will work?"

"I have no idea, Watson, but we are running short of time, so I rather think desperate measures are called for. Another advantage we have is the fact that Mycroft can be quite convincing when he wishes."

The next day was singularly uneventful. I must admit that my thoughts were preoccupied with our pending meeting with Mycroft. Holmes was in and out of our lodgings several times, and all my inquiries were politely rebuffed.

Finally, after we had dined, my friend glanced at his watch and said, "It is now 6:30. The weather is quite pleasant. Shall we walk to the Diogenes?"

Having remained indoors all day, I readily assented. Grabbing out hats and sticks, we set out for Pall Mall. I considered pressing Holmes as we walked and then decided against it, reasoning I would know all soon enough.

After arriving at the Diogenes, we were shown into the Stranger's Room. We were offered refreshments, which we declined, and after a few minutes, Holmes glanced at his watch. "As you know, Watson, Mycroft is a creature of unvarying habits. It is now 7 o'clock."

"Perhaps he is running late or was delayed at his office."

"If that were the case, Mycroft would have sent a message or phoned the Diogenes to inform us of his tardiness. I must confess to harboring certain misgivings."

"Holmes," I exclaimed, looking at my own watch, "it is but two minutes past the hour. Surely, with the conference so close, there are any number of things that might have delayed your brother."

Summoning one of the valets, Holmes was informed that Mycroft had not visited the club all day.

Turning to me, he said, "Let us walk the route that Mycroft traverses each day. Perhaps we shall encounter him along the way."

So we set out for Mycroft's office in Whitehall. Although the building was largely empty, the receptionist informed us that he had come on duty at 5 o'clock and, although he might have missed him, he could not recall seeing Mr. Holmes leave the building.

We also learned that Mycroft's quartet of assistants had all left between 5 and 6 o'clock.

Next, we retraced our steps to Pall Mall and stopped by Mycroft's flat, which was quite near the

Diogenes Club. His rooms appeared dark from the street and our knocks on the door went unanswered.

"What do you make of this unexplained delay?" I asked Holmes.

"Given the rather circumscribed orbit in which Mycroft moves, his absence from all his usual haunts gives me pause."

"Let us return to the Diogenes Club," I suggested. "Perhaps Mycroft arrived while we were away."

Reluctantly, Holmes agreed. So it was a few minutes later that we found ourselves once again ensconced in the Stranger's Room. The same valet, who had attended us a short time earlier, entered the room after a brief wait. He was carrying a small, silver tray with a letter on it.

"This was delivered by messenger while you were gone," he said, handing Holmes the envelope.

Taking the missive, Holmes examined the paper carefully. Looking at me, he said, "It is addressed to me although it is not Mycroft's hand."

Withdrawing a penknife from his pocket, Holmes carefully slit the envelope open; he withdrew a single sheet of paper that had been folded in half. Opening it, he perused it several times.

Unable to contain my curiosity any longer, I finally exclaimed, "Holmes, what does it say?"

He handed me the note, "I had but to read the first four words to grasp the import. The message began:

"We have your brother."

Chapter 11

"Who would do this, Holmes?"

"Obviously, someone who doesn't want the peace conference to succeed," he replied.

My mind was racing. While I had some grasp of the political ramifications of the conference, I must admit to being more than a bit naïve regarding many of the finer points. I knew that the Germans and Austrians seemed to be determined to dominate Europe. However, I also understood that given our isolation, Britain need not be drawn into the conflict which now seemed certain to erupt in the very near future. However, our alliances seemed to run counter to my theory of isolationism.

"Then we must locate your brother and set things right."

"Have you read the entire letter?" asked Holmes. I shook my head and returned to the missive which I still clutched in my hand.

"You will remove yourself from the situation. Any interference on your part – and we will brook

none – places your brother's life
at risk."

As you might expect, the letter was not signed.

"What's to be done?" I asked.

"Since I have been ordered to 'remove' myself – a phrase with which I am all too familiar – you must once again act in my stead. If they believe that I am sitting out this affair, safely ensconced in our lodgings, you should have free rein to do what needs to be done throughout the city. However, I should caution you that you will no doubt be under constant surveillance, so you must place a premium on discretion."

"You know that you can count on me, Holmes."

"Well, there is little that we can accomplish this evening. Tomorrow, after breakfast, the first thing you must do is seek out Wiggins and see if he has anything to report about Mycroft's assistants – Geoffrey Langlois, Diedrich Bern, Deniz Cenk, and Alexander Dennison."

"You really believe one of them may be a spy?"

"I certainly hope not, but at this point, all indications lead to that conclusion."

"Where am I to locate Wiggins?"

Holmes then rattled off a list of locations known to be frequented by the leader of the Irregulars, "I would start with the market and then the shop owned by his uncle. After you have located him, tell him we need to double our surveillance of the aides. It is imperative that I know their various locations every minute of the day."

"And you will spend the entire day at Baker Street?"

"I did not say that," replied Holmes with a smile. "There is one important call that I must make, and I am rather hoping it may shed some new light on this rather dark situation."

The next morning Holmes reiterated his instructions to me. "And remember, Watson, you must be the very soul of discretion."

After walking a few blocks and making certain that I was not being followed, I hailed a hansom and set out for the Portobello Road Market, hoping for a bit of luck. Holmes had informed me that Wiggins often helped out at a stall there that was owned by his family. Apparently, it was central enough that it also served him well as a sort of clearinghouse in his myriad endeavors for Holmes.

After arriving at the market, perhaps London's oldest, it took me some ten minutes to find the stall. I was in luck, although Wiggins spotted me before I saw him, and I heard a voice exclaim, "Dr. Watson, are you doin' the shoppin' now? I thought that was Mrs. 'Udson's job. "

"I am here on behalf of Mr. Holmes," I said.

"I rather suspected that," replied Wiggins, "Is 'e checkin' on 'is brother's assistants again?"

"Yes, you have had members of the Irregulars following them?"

"'Deed we 'ave," said Wiggins. "None of the blokes have been out of our sight except when they're indoors."

"Have the Irregulars following them noticed anything unusual about any of the four?"

"Not really, Doctor. Two of them – Bern and Dennison – live in Mayfair and a third – Langlois – has a flat near Fitzrovia. Cenk lives in Marylebone, not too far from you and Mr. 'Olmes. They all walk from their flats to work every day. For the most part, they're rather retiring gents. They do go out at night occasionally, but more often than not, they stay in. Rather a boring life, if you ask me."

"And the Irregulars have noticed nothing out of the ordinary?"

"Not unless you consider stoppin' in a park for a smoke unusual."

"What do you mean?"

"As I told Mr. 'Olmes a few days ago, just about every night, Langlois, who 'as a flat in Alfred Mews walks to one of the nearby parks on 'is way home. Once there, 'e sits on a bench, reads 'is paper and enjoys a cigarette or a cigar before heading for 'is flat."

"Perhaps he just enjoys the fresh air? Perhaps he is not allowed to smoke in his rooms?"

Wiggins gave me a look which I found difficult to interpret, but it was obvious he placed far more importance on Langlois' daily visits to a park than I did. "Does he ever meet with anyone?" I asked.

"Not that we've seen so far. He sits, enjoys his smoke while he reads the paper and then leaves the park."

"Anything else?"

"Maybe," replied Wiggins enigmatically. "He always sits on one of two benches, and it strikes me as rather odd."

"Why do you say that?"

"Because there's never anyone else around. He could 'ave the same seat every day, but 'e doesn't. I find that a bit peculiar."

"Perhaps," I said, humoring Wiggins. "I will make a point of passing along your observations to Mr. Holmes. And what of the other three?"

"Even more borin' than this bloke. They work and go home. A few nights the Bern fella went to a pub for dinner, and on another night Cenk went to the theatre with his wife and to the park with 'is sons; otherwise, they eat in their rooms as well." He paused then repeated the sentiment he had expressed earlier, "Not much of a life if you ask me."

"Well, you and your band seem to have everything under control. I shall make a full report to Mr. Holmes, extolling your diligence."

On my way back to Baker Street, I considered paying a visit to Lestrade. I finally decided against it as I had no news to report – at least none that would bolster the little detective's spirits.

When I finally reached our lodgings, I was surprised to discover that Holmes was conspicuously absent. I was just about to ask Mrs. Hudson if she knew where he had gone – though Holmes seldom shared his itinerary with anyone – when I heard the bell chime.

A minute or so later, Mrs. Hudson knocked on the door and announced, "Inspector Lestrade is here to see Mr. Holmes."

"Holmes is not here," I replied, "but do show the Inspector up, and if you would prepare a pot of coffee that would be much appreciated."

She nodded her assent and left the room. A minute later, Lestrade entered and I greeted him warmly. After we had exchanged pleasantries, Lestrade said, "Mr. Holmes asked me to meet him here at noon. I realize I am a bit early, but I must confess to being somewhat eager to hear what he has to say."

"I can certainly appreciate your anxiety, Lestrade, and I wish there were something I could do to ease your concerns, but you know how close-mouthed Holmes is. He has shared little with me. The only thing I know for certain is that your case is connected to one, or perhaps two others, which Holmes is investigating."

"Mr. Holmes had mentioned my difficulty might be linked to other cases. Do tell me more, Dr. Watson."

Not knowing how much Holmes would be willing to divulge about the various cases – including the sudden disappearance of his brother – I decided that putting Lestrade off might be the best course of action. "I should like to enlighten you, Inspector, but I am not conversant with all the details. To that end, I suggest we wait for Holmes."

"I understand," replied Lestrade, winking at me, "even if I don't believe you, Doctor Watson." At that we both chuckled and the conversation soon turned to other things. However, after a prolonged silence, Lestrade stated, "I understand why I have been suspended; I just hope Mr. Holmes is able to clear my name." Growing a bit more animated, he continued, "I have had a long and successful career, thanks in no small part to the aid I received from the both of you. I would just like the opportunity to leave on my own terms – if I must."

Just as the Inspector had finished speaking, the door flew open and in walked Holmes, who proclaimed, "And so you shall, Lestrade, so you shall."

"Mr. Holmes," said the inspector, how good to see you."

"We can share pleasantries later, Lestrade. Right now, we must get to work."

"Righto," said the policeman. "What's to be done?"

Setting a rather large, thick parcel wrapped in brown paper on the floor beside his chair, Holmes turned to Lestrade and said, "I firmly believe that your suspension was a clever attempt to occupy me while other events were taking place. In short, Lestrade, your smuggling ring was probably a cleverly developed hoax, designed to lead to your suspension and thus incommode me from pursuing another investigation as I labored to clear your name."

"What's it all about?" asked Lestrade. "Dr. Watson reiterated what you had told me – that my suspension might be linked to one or two of your other cases." At that Holmes shot me a look. Taking note, Lestrade continued, "But he hasn't told me anything beyond that, Mr. Holmes. It appears that he can be as tight-lipped as you when he chooses."

At that Holmes laughed, looked at me and said, "Well done, Watson."

Turning to Lestrade, he said, "I am going to need your help."

"You know you have it, Mr. Holmes."

"What I am about to tell you must remain top-secret for the time being. When the time is right, I hope to resolve a number of cases simultaneously. After, you may have all the credit, which, if nothing else, should serve to quash any thoughts of terminating your tenure at the Yard. In fact, I hope to be able to prove that the smuggling ring and attempt to besmirch your good name were nothing more than minor elements in an elaborate plot."

"But to what end?" pleaded Lestrade.

Holmes then proceeded to tell Lestrade everything about the missing manuscript, the safe and the desk. Upon being told that his name had been forged at the furniture factory, Lestrade nearly became apoplectic. Holmes concluded by informing him about the peace conference and the abduction of Mycroft before concluding with summaries of the four assistants, including Langlois' daily visits to the park.

After he had finished," he turned to me and asked, "Watson, you have just spoken with Wiggins. Has he anything new to add?"

"No, I think you have summed it up quite nicely, Holmes."

"You certainly have a great many things to occupy your time," said Lestrade. "Obviously Mycroft's situation and the pending peace conference are far more concerning than my own."

Although Holmes is never emotional, I thought I detected a faint smile of gratitude play across his face for a second. "Thank you, Lestrade, but that is simply not the case; all that has transpired in the past few weeks is merely the tip of the iceberg. There is a great deal hidden beneath the surface that we must somehow bring to light. I believe Mycroft's assistant Langlois is involved, but I do not think he is the mastermind – and that is the person we must discover and unmask."

"How can you be certain that Langlois isn't behind everything?" I asked.

"His daily trips to the park. I have seen him there thrice. Sometimes he smokes a cigarette; other times, he smokes a cigar."

"As do you and I," I replied.

"Yes, but Langlois sometimes arrives at the park with a newspaper while at other times, he enters empty-handed and yet leaves with a paper which he has picked up."

"He's communicating with someone," exclaimed Lestrade.

I couldn't believe Lestrade had arrived at the conclusion before I had, and I was also berating myself for not taking Wiggins' observations more seriously.

"Bravo, Lestrade. Yes, they are using quite an ingenious code for their messages," said Holmes. He then glanced at me and asked, "Is anything wrong, Watson?"

"Now all we have to do is find out with whom he is communicating," added the little detective. I was never so glad for the distraction as I was at that moment.

"There's a bit more to it than that, Inspector. We must also learn how the code they are using works. Fortunately, I have already begun that process," said Holmes.

"Now Lestrade, here is what I will need you to do. After I have solved the riddle posed by the code, which is proving to be no easy task, I am going to call upon you to play a role in following whoever it is that retrieves Langlois' next message or perhaps you will be tasked with tailing Langlois himself."

"I am at your service, Mr. Holmes. Just let me know where and when I need to be."

"Thank you, Inspector."

"It is I who should be thanking you Mr. Holmes. Without your help, I'd be off the force for certain."

"Well, we are not in the clear yet, Lestrade, but I do believe things may be looking up."

With that the Inspector shook our hands and departed.

After he had left, I said to Holmes, "He really is quite grateful, you know?"

However, Holmes either did not hear me or decided to ignore that remark; I rather suspect it was the latter.

After informing me that he would need quiet as he intended to resume working on the cipher, I asked, "How on Earth did you discover the type of code they are using?"

Holmes smiled, "That was the easiest part of all. I had one of the Irregulars snatch the paper Langlois had discarded before anyone else could get to it."

"And what did you discover?" I asked.

"That's the deuce of it, Watson. I am certain they are using some variant of a Caesar cipher code, but I have tried every possible substitution without the slightest bit of success."

"A Caesar cipher code?" I asked.

"Yes, on the surface, it is actually quite a simple substitution code. You and your partner agree on a predetermined number, and then every letter moves that many places down in the alphabet. For instance, if the number were six, then F would be A, and G would be B and so on. If the number were 10, J would be A, K would be B, and so on all the way through."

"You say you've tried various substitutions? How did you determine the number?"

"All the underlined letters appeared on Page 6 of The Times. I started with that as the key, but when I made the substitutions, using F as A, it was obvious that some other letter was serving as the key. I then tried reversing it with similar results."

"Perhaps the message has been cast in a foreign language. Possibly German or Russian?"

"I have tried translating it into French and German. I'm afraid that Russian is out of the question, given the Cyrillic alphabet."

"Oh?" I said, not wanting to admit I knew precious little about the Russian language.

"Yes, you see, the Cyrillic alphabet consists of 33 letters, divided into 10 vowels, 21 consonants and 2 letters which do not designate any sounds, so I think we can safely rule out the language of the czars."

"Well then, Holmes, the only thing I can suggest is that you employ the talents of a linguistic scholar."

Holmes looked at me dumbfounded. "That's it, Watson. How could I have been so dense!"

"What is it?" I asked befuddled.

"I do not require a linguistic scholar – but the language of scholars. The message must be written in Latin. Give me a moment here." He worked on the code for a several minutes and then threw up his hands in exasperation. "That makes no sense either. I must be missing something, and it must be fairly evident. Something so obvious that I am overlooking it."

Knowing my friend would be best served by my leaving him in silence, I retired to my chair and began reading and smoking my pipe. I had been at it for perhaps thirty minutes when I heard Holmes exclaim, "Eureka!"

"Have you solved it then?"

"Indeed! I have been staring at the key the entire time, but it was hiding in plain sight."

"And what gave it away?"

"I kept thinking Latin? Why Latin? There must be something. Remember I told you the letters were on Page 6. Well, the first letter underlined was X, which if the key started with F, for page six, as A would make V read as M and the next underlined letter, A, read as J. That told me immediately I had erred. I then tried moving one letter in front and then one behind, but both attempts also proved fruitless. I then remembered that X is also the Latin for 10, so I tried moving ten letters in either direction, and again, the results yielded nonsense.

"Finally, it struck me that perhaps X was the key, so I started by eliminating the first ten underlined letters while keeping J, the tenth letter, as my A. Now the message began with an O, which will become F when we are finished.

"After several minutes, I had finally completed the first transcription, the message read OCLVEWRWXTTLABDVVRQRQALWXTCNJMX LCX." He then showed me the paper with the indecipherable string of letters.

172

"Why Holmes, that's nothing more than gibberish, sheer nonsense."

"In English yes, it certainly appears that way. However, if you now translate the letters a second time into Latin, again using J as A you end up with FLUMENINOCCURSUMMIHIACNOCTEADOCTO. Fortunately, they eschewed the classical Latin alphabet, having need of U in this message and probably the W and V in other communiqués.

"Does that help?"

After studying the letters for a moment or two, I replied "Not terribly."

"See if you can manage to break it up into smaller, more manageable fragments, Watson."

"Well, I believe I can discern *octo* or eight at the end there."

"Excellent! Anything else?"

"I can also see the *ad* or at right before that, but I am afraid my Latin is far more rusty than yours."

"Consider FLUMEN IN OCCURSUM MIHI HAC NOCTE AD OCTO or 'Meet me at the river tonight at eight.'"

"Bravo, Holmes! But since this paper is several days old, how valuable is that message?"

"It's extremely important in that it provides us with the key to their code. I am certain that pilfering this paper slowed them down for a day or two and perhaps caused a small degree of consternation."

"I agree," I said, "but what is your next move? The conference is scheduled to begin the day after tomorrow and, from what you have told me, without Mycroft there is no conference."

"So then it falls to us to try to delay the conference for at least a day or two, perhaps longer if need be?"

"To what end?"

"So that I may send a message of my own to those who have abducted my brother and, with any luck, learn who is responsible for this interference in the affairs of England."

"But how will you do it?" I asked.

"There are several possibilities. I shall let you know as soon as I determine a precise course of action. I have a few ideas but they will require sorting out."

He paused and then continued, "In the meantime, Watson, I must request your indulgence.

"You have but to ask, old friend."

Holmes then gave me a very precise set of instructions that began with my once again visiting the British Museum and the nearby bookshop owned by Madame Cocilovo-Kozzi and finally reuniting with Lestrade before meeting Holmes at a prearranged time and location.

Chapter 12

Since time was of the essence, I hailed a cab and told the driver there was an extra sovereign in it for him if he could get me to the British Museum post-haste. We sped along Marylebone Road and then turned onto Gower Street; in less than a quarter hour, I had arrived at the museum.

I asked the guard if he knew if Dr. Smith were in. After a short phone call, he informed me that he was, and I was on my way to his office before the guard had even begun to give me directions.

"Dr. Watson, this is a surprise," said Smith as I was led into his office. "Is Mr. Holmes not with you?"

"He is quite occupied at the moment, but he wanted me to examine something in the King's Library."

"Has he located the *Beowulf* manuscript?" asked Smith anxiously.

"I believe he has made significant progress," I replied.

Seeing the crestfallen look on the scholar's face, I was tempted to tell him the truth, but I steeled myself and did what I could to alleviate his obvious anxiety. "You know that Mr. Holmes promised he would find the manuscript, and in our long association, I have never known him to break a promise."

A smile returned to his face as we walked towards the rare book room. Smith nodded to the guard as he admitted us, and when we were inside, he asked, "Is there anything that I can assist you with, Dr. Watson?"

"I wonder if I might have a cup of tea while I work."

As soon as Smith had left to fetch the tea, I set about the task Holmes had assigned me. While I saw any number of volumes that appeared suitable, given the attributes which Holmes had told me the book must possess; ultimately, I followed his directions and settled on an oversized two-volume edition of Dr. Johnson's Dictionary. Wrestling the second volume, as he had instructed me to do, from the shelf, I placed it on the closest table and had just finished measuring it when I heard Dr. Smith at the door.

He entered carrying a small tray with two cups, which he placed on the table next to the one on which I had placed the Dictionary.

"No point in taking chances," said Smith. Then looking at the volume, he inquired, "Dr. Johnson's Dictionary?"

"It may be relevant to the case, and I am afraid that is all I can say for the moment?"

He nodded and then said, "I am familiar with the methods employed by Mr. Holmes."

As we enjoyed the tea, we chatted about various things. I asked Smith, "Is this the biggest book in this room?"

He replied, "It depends upon how you define 'biggest.' If you mean in terms of size, the dictionary is certainly one of the larger items, if not the largest, in the collection. Taken together, the two volumes weigh more than a stone and a half. However, they may seem small when you consider that the first edition of Samuel Richardson's *Clarissa, or, the History of a Young Lady*, has seven volumes with nearly 300 more pages and weighs just slightly more." With that he pointed to a shelf, where I could see the work in question. Although the books were smaller, they still looked rather formidable.

Having acquired the necessary information, I chatted with Dr. Smith a while longer and then replaced the book, thanking him for his assistance as I did so.

"I am not quite certain that I have done anything to earn your gratitude, but you are always welcome here Dr. Watson – with or without Mr. Holmes."

I then left the Museum and made my way to the bookstore owned by Madame Cocilovo-Kozzi and her husband. She greeted me at the door and invited me in. "Would you care for some tea?" she asked.

I replied that ordinarily I would but that I had just enjoyed a cup at the museum. Remembering the importance of time, I said, "I understand you have something for me."

With that she turned and called for her husband, "Jonathan, Dr. Watson is here, and he seems in a bit of a hurry."

While I was marveling at her deduction, her spouse entered the room, carrying a small bundle that had been wrapped in brown butcher's paper and secured with heavy twine. I could tell from the shape that it was a book, so I decided to throw caution to the wind. "That's not the *Beowulf* manuscript, is it?" I asked excitedly.

They looked at each other and began laughing. When they had regained their composure, Jonathan looked at me and asked, "Do you really think I would treat one of England's greatest treasures in such a cavalier manner? No, Doctor, this is not the *Nowell Codex*. This is merely a copy of Samuel Butler's *Erewhon*, though why Mr. Holmes has requested such a thing baffles the two of us. However, you may assure Mr. Holmes that it meets all the specifications which he supplied."

"Samuel Butler? How very odd!"

"I don't think it is the book that is important to Mr. Holmes, so much as its attributes."

"Attributes?"

"Indeed. He was very specific in requesting a book of a certain weight and dimensions. He also indicated that a book by Butler would be preferable. Although it took some time, I finally stumbled across this first edition of *Erewhon* which seems to fit the bill nicely."

Totally baffled as to what Holmes might have in mind, I nevertheless thanked the couple and then hailed a cab for Cleveland Street, where I planned to rendezvous with Lestrade.

During the ride I reflected on the many twists and turns this case had taken so far. Although we had crossed swords and matched wits with any number of formidable opponents, including the late, unlamented Professor Moriarty, this case seemed far more pressing, especially when one considered the abduction of Mycroft and the possible threat to the very fragile peace in Europe.

I had the driver leave me at the intersection of Cleveland Street and Grafton Way. No sooner had I descended than I spotted Lestrade, leaning against a lamppost, smoking a cigar. Crossing to him, I asked, "Have you heard from Holmes?"

"Not yet," replied Lestrade. "I was rather hoping you might know what he was planning."

I looked at my watch and said, "Well, we are on time. Holmes said to be here at five, and it is one minute before the hour."

At that point, a young costermonger approached us. He was obviously looking to unload some of the fruit he carried in a tray that hung in front of him, supported by a strap that crossed his shoulders in the back. "Care for an apple, sir. They are quite fresh and delicious."

"No, thank you," I replied.

"I think you should at least examine them, sir. They were picked just this morning."

"Listen," said Lestrade gruffly, "the gentleman said he doesn't care for one. So why don't you just move along?"

"They're free for the police," replied the lad, and lowering his voice, he added, "and for residents of Baker Street."

As you might expect I was quite taken aback by the young man's words. Realizing that he was a messenger from Holmes, I asked, "And which would you suggest?"

He selected two from the tray and placed them in a paper sack. "Be very careful," he cautioned, "these sacks sometimes rip." With that he started off down the street, hawking his wares much like any other street vendor.

"Obviously, he was sent by Holmes," Lestrade offered, "but to what end?"

"I am not quite certain, I replied, "Fancy an apple?"

Lestrade declined, but I was quite hungry, so I reached into the sack and that was when I noticed the drawing. Trying to appear unobtrusive, I studied the diagram that had been drawn in pencil on the sack and soon realized it was a crude map of Fitzroy Square Park. There was a circle which represented the garden in the center of the park, surrounded by a square, which was intended to depict the streets.

I saw an "L" and a "G" on one side of the square and a "W" and an "F" on the other. At the very top of the bag was written "G.L. – 5:15."

Since we were still a block from the park, I said to Lestrade, "I think we've received our instructions from Holmes."

Showing him the map, I indicated the letters and said, "If I am reading this correctly, I am to take up a position near the entrance on Fitzroy Street while you are to assume a similar spot near the gate on Grafton Way."

"And who are we looking for? And what are we to do when we see the individual in question?"

"The first part is easy. We are to be on the lookout for one Geoffrey Langlois, one of Mycroft's aides. I then described Langlois to Lestrade. "Well-dressed, rather tall and thin with a beard, you say?" I nodded. "Well, that eliminates about three quarters of the males in London," he remarked.

Remembering what Wiggins had told me, I added, "He will stop in the park and sit on a bench to smoke and read a newspaper."

"Well that certainly helps," replied Lestrade. "But what are we to do once we spot him?"

"We are to watch him and see if he meets with anyone."

"And when he leaves the park?" asked Lestrade.

"Unless we hear from Holmes, I think we should try to follow him. If he meets with someone, you follow Langlois, and I will tail the other party. I know he has a flat right around here, not too far from Cleveland Street, so, depending upon what happens, you or the two of us can follow him home."

"Seems like a lot of effort expended for nothing," said Lestrade.

"You know how mysterious Holmes can be," I remarked.

"True enough," observed the Inspector, "and one certainly can't take issue with his results."

Looking at my watch, I said, "We need to get to our places. When I see Langlois enter the park, I will take off my hat. The arm I use to remove my hat will indicate the side Langlois is taking around the circle."

"I will be keeping an eye on you, Dr. Watson."

With that, we parted company. I walked down Conroy Street, preparing to find a bench near the Fitzroy Street entrance. I purchased a paper from a youngster who was bellowing, "Fire in the East End," so that I might have something to hide behind should it become necessary. After all, I reasoned, Langlois had seen my face and was aware I was friends with Holmes.

I found a seat on a bench, but before I sat, I made certain that I could see Lestrade at the other end of the park. I was wondering if he would be able to spot my signal when he suddenly lifted his hat, and I understood he could see me as well. Sitting down, I opened the paper and pretended to read, all the while keeping a watch for the approach of Langlois.

Since it was a warm summer evening, the park was somewhat crowded as workers made their way home or met other workers, friends or members of the opposite sex – perhaps for a pint or a light supper. As I was sitting there, I saw an ancient violinist making his way about the park, playing various songs for different people. He had a cup hanging from his neck and was obviously performing in hopes of earning a few coins. I wondered to myself if the musician might be Holmes in disguise, but then I realized that he had but one leg and was assisted by a large wooden crutch which he kept propped under his left arm while playing. I also thought he appeared too short to be Holmes.

I was so preoccupied in watching the musician and marveling at his dexterity that I nearly missed

Langlois as he entered the park on my right. I quickly snapped my paper up, and after he had walked past me, I watched him take a seat about midway up on the side of the park. I stood and quickly raised my hat with my left hand, smoothing my hair with my right. When I saw Lestrade return the signal, I was immediately relieved.

From behind my paper, I watched as Langlois snipped the end off a cigar and lit it before snapping open his own paper. He sat there for some five minutes and then he folded up his paper, placed it on the bench and began walking in the direction of Lestrade. As he headed towards the Inspector, I fell in some twenty or thirty feet behind him. As I drew close to the bench where he had been sitting, I saw the paper was still there. I decided to retrieve the newspaper he had left behind. I felt certain its contents would prove invaluable to my old friend. I was about ten feet from the bench and preparing to retrieve the paper, when I heard a woman scream.

Looking back, I saw the violinist laying on the ground, writhing in agony. "Is there a doctor here?" someone yelled.

I was torn: On the one hand, I was determined to help Holmes and possibly free Mycroft, but at the same time, I had sworn an oath. I decided the paper could wait a few minutes while I tended to the stricken musician. Turning back, I loudly announced, "I am a doctor." I then rushed to the man and examined him. His pulse was strong, although he was apparently unconscious. "Give him air," I said, waving everyone back.

I could discern no obvious injuries, and was about to rise when I felt a vise-like grip on my right wrist. I almost bellowed out loud, but as I glanced at the weathered face on the ground before me, I thought I saw the man wink at me. At that moment, realization flooded over me, and I felt as though I might have turned crimson with embarrassment – and anger.

I said to those nearby, "He's coming around now, but he has had a nasty fall." As he sat up, all those in the vicinity began to place coins in the cup around his neck. As he struggled to rise on his one visible leg, the violinist thanked those around him and said with a heavy Italian accent, "Grazie! Grazie! My crutch, she slip on something, and when I fall, I crack my head," He then began to play a medley of pieces, at which everyone applauded.

Leaving Holmes in the park, I headed for the bench where I was stunned to discover that the paper was no longer there. Deciding there was little else to be done, I looked about for Lestrade, and not seeing him, decided it might be best if I returned home. I was still furious with Holmes about the deception, but as I walked my anger began to abate, and by the time I had reached the front door of 221B, I was almost in complete control of my emotions.

After placing the copy of *Erewhon* on his chair, I waited for Holmes to return. After an hour had passed, I dined alone and was glad I had, for it was well past seven when I heard my friend's tread on the stairs. As he entered, still dressed as the ancient violinist – only now with two legs. I watched in silence as he limped across the room, picked up the book I had left on his cushion and placed it on the floor on top of the larger parcel he had placed there some days earlier, He then threw himself into his favorite chair. Unable to restrain myself any longer, I exclaimed, "My word, it's a miracle. You can walk!"

"Just barely," he replied, rubbing his leg.

"How did you manage it? Leg bent at the knee and secured to your thigh?"

"Exactly. Cover everything with oversized pants pinned up on one side and a longer coat and the illusion is complete."

I then returned to the paper which I hadn't really been reading. After a few seconds, Holmes laughed and his chuckling only hastened the return of my anger. Then to my surprise, he said, "I cannot blame you for being put out, but it was imperative that things unfold in a very specific manner."

"With me making a fool of myself in the park?"

"No," replied Holmes, "with you following Lestrade, who was following Langlois."

"Well, Lestrade may have tailed him, but I certainly didn't."

"Watson, I know you meant well. I should have foreseen you thinking I might have found Langlois' newspaper useful."

"Indeed, you have cracked the code. You would have been able to decipher their latest message and perhaps that might have provided some clue as to the whereabouts of your brother."

Pulling a paper from inside his coat, Holmes smiled and said, "I have already done both those things."

"But how?" I spluttered.

"The Irregulars. You see I had prepared two papers – The Times and The Telegraph – and as soon as I saw Langlois enter the park, I signaled the lad with the Times. Had you retrieved Langlois' paper, you would have thrown a spanner in the works for certain, so I had to resort to the histrionics to distract you and allow my copy of The Times to be substituted for the one Langlois had brought."

"And what did his message say?"

"He reported that the conference is definitely scheduled to begin the day after tomorrow at the Marble Arch at 9 a.m."

"And what did your message say?"

"Urgent we meet tomorrow, first gallery, St. Paul's, 9:15."

"Do you know with whom you will be meeting?"

"Unless I am quite mistaken, it will be with one Otto Kueck, a member of the *Ettappendienst der Marine*, a sort of German secret service."

"The Germans always seem to be ahead of us when it comes to spying. From what you say, they appear to have a special branch devoted to it. Certainly, we should pursue a similar course of action."

Peering at me, Holmes simply remarked, "Perhaps we already do."

Although I pressed Holmes on that point, he remained adamant, refusing to elaborate in any way. Finally, in an effort to change the subject, he said, "I have to go out tonight. Would you care to accompany me?"

"Where are we going?" I asked, my anger now totally eclipsed by the opportunity to join Holmes in the hunt.

"I think it is about time we rescued Mycroft, don't you? After all, the peace conference begins the day after tomorrow and I am certain he will need some time to recuperate and prepare."

"You mean you know where your brother is being held?"

"Not quite yet, but I believe I shall in a very short time. Now, just let me change my clothes and clean up a bit and we shall be on our way."

"Would it do any good to ask where we are going?"

"Certainly you can figure that out on your own, Watson." With that parting remark, he vanished into his room, and I was left to my own devices, trying to think as Holmes thought and see what he had seen. As you might expect, I soon found myself woefully out of my depth.

Chapter 13

After some twenty minutes, Holmes reappeared looking much like himself although I thought I could still discern a slight limp.

"Come on, old fellow. Grab your coat. And if you would be so kind, perhaps you would bring your service revolver as well."

After fetching my pistol, I descended the stairs to discover that Holmes had already hailed a cab. Soon I realized we were headed in the general direction of the British Museum. "Are we going to see Dr. Smith?" I asked.

Holmes chuckled, "I told you we were going to free Mycroft."

A few minutes later, the cab stopped and we alighted at the intersection of Tottenham Court Road and Torrington Place. When we descended, I noticed Lestrade standing by a gate in the middle of the block, near Alfred Mews. As we approached, he said, "You certainly took your time getting here."

"It couldn't be avoided," said Holmes. "How is Langlois?"

"He went straight home from the park, and, as far as I can tell, he hasn't budged from his flat since."

"You're certain?" asked Holmes.

"No one has gone in or out of the front door while I have been here. I don't know for certain if there is another entrance, but I imagine there must be."

"There were supposed to be two of you here just in case of that eventuality," replied Holmes, casting a quick glance in my direction. "Which is his flat?"

"Number 1, ground floor on the right," replied Lestrade.

"Since you are the only one with any legal standing, Inspector, would you care to accompany us?"

"I have no legal standing," replied Lestrade, "I'm still suspended."

"Yes, but Langlois does not know that," replied Holmes.

"In for a penny, in for a pound," replied Lestrade. "There's little else they can do to me, I suppose."

"That's the spirit," said Holmes in a rather cajoling tone of voice.

Lestrade turned his back and kept guard while Holmes picked the front door lock. Once inside, we made our way to the flat. Lestrade stood on one side of the door and I on the other. Holmes knocked and said, "Mr. Langlois, it is Sherlock Holmes; I have come to talk to you about my brother's disappearance."

His announcement was greeted by silence. He rapped on the door again and repeated himself. Once more, stillness reigned.

"You want me to kick it in?" asked Lestrade.

"That won't be necessary, Inspector." Holmes again withdrew the small leather case from his pocket, and after selecting a lock pick, he worked his magic and some ten seconds later, he was pushing open the door to Langlois' rooms. "Mr. Langlois?"

Upon receiving no answer, Holmes entered the flat, followed by Lestrade while I brought up the rear.

We were greeted by the rather macabre sight of Geoffrey Langlois, sitting at his table, ready to enjoy a dinner of bangers and mash – the only thing preventing him was the fact that his head was hanging at an unnatural angle because he was dead.

"What do you make of it, Watson?"

After a quick examination, I said, "I cannot be certain without a proper post-mortem, but I should think that his larynx was crushed and then his neck was snapped. He may not have died immediately, but the crushed larynx would have prevented him from calling out."

Turning to Lestrade, Holmes said, "You saw no one enter or exit the building after Langlois?"

"At least not through the front door," said Lestrade.

"See if there is a back entrance which our killer could have employed."

After Lestrade had left, Holmes said, "We have only a few minutes before the Inspector's return. Stand by the door and when you hear him coming back, go into the hall and delay him."

"What am I to say?

"I will leave that to your imagination," said Holmes. Touching the food on the plate, he observed, "It is still slightly warm, so we did not miss our killer by much."

"Why did they kill him?"

"Perhaps they realized we had solved the code. Perhaps they were afraid he would talk. It is difficult to say without facts at our disposal, Watson."

As we spoke, Holmes began examining the few books on the shelves and then he turned his attention to the desk.

At that moment, I thought I heard Lestrade in the hall. Leaving Holmes to his own devices, I stepped outside where the Inspector was heading towards me from the back of the house.

"Is there a rear entrance, Inspector?"

"Yes, it opens onto an alleyway that leads to a backyard with a gate and a passageway to Huntley Street."

As he tried to move past me, I said, "Holmes thought we should check the first and second floors – and possibly the roof. Just in case …"

"I hardly think…" Lestrade started to respond, but I cut him off as I brushed by him and started up the staircase. Thankfully, he soon fell in behind me as I had hoped he might. As expected, the upper floors yielded nothing, nor did the roof.

As we descended, Lestrade remarked, "I tried to tell you this was a waste of time."

"Perhaps," said Holmes stepping from Langlois' room, "but one must never leave any stone unturned."

"And what are we to do now?" asked Lestrade.

"I think you should report the murder to the nearest constable. Tell him the killer is approximately six feet tall, powerfully built and quite strong. He has light blonde hair, almost white, walks with a pronounced limp of the left leg and is probably Slavic or Russian. That information will not get you your job back just yet, Lestrade, but it may help at some point in the future. Watson and I are returning to Baker Street. Contact me there if you should require anything else."

As we started to leave, Holmes turned back to Lestrade and said, "One more thing, Inspector."

"Oh?"

"I would urge you to keep this discovery as quiet as possible. If you can withhold the identity of the victim for a day or two that would help immeasurably."

"I will do my best, Mr. Holmes, even if I have to call in a few favors."

"Thank you, Inspector, and by the way, well done today. Your assistance has proven invaluable."

After we had hailed a cab and given the driver our address, I said to Holmes, "What amazing deductions you arrived at regarding Langlois' killer. They should go a long way in helping the Yard apprehend him."

"I rather doubt that," replied Holmes.

"Oh? Why do you say that?"

"Truth be told, I made most of that up."

"What?! Why on Earth would you do that?"

"Until we have freed Mycroft, I simply cannot take a chance that Lestrade and his cohorts will stumble across the truth. Better, I think to point them in an entirely different direction than to have them inadvertently blunder into my carefully laid plans."

"So then you did learn something while I was distracting Lestrade."

"Let us say that I made three rather interesting discoveries. Shall I enumerate them for you?"

"By all means," I exclaimed.

"First, I discovered three distinct types of ash in the soup bowl which Langlois had been employing as an ashtray. Second, the keys to the flat door were still in Langlois' jacket pocket. Third, inside a leather case in his jacket pocket, I discovered a rather strong pair of reading glasses."

"That's it?!" I exclaimed. "You learned that he was a heavy smoker with poor eyesight."

"Don't forget the keys, Watson," said Holmes soothingly, "I find that fact perhaps most telling of all."

As we pulled up in front of our lodgings, I admitted to Holmes that I was totally baffled. "It seems to me that for all the progress we appear to have made, we are right back at the beginning. Our primary suspect has been murdered; both Mycroft and *Cotton Vitellius A XV* are still missing; the smugglers have not been captured; and Lestrade remains suspended."

"Those are all things I hope to rectify in the very near future," said Holmes as we entered our rooms. "Now, would you care for a nightcap? We have an important appointment at St. Paul's in the morning."

In all the excitement I had quite forgot about Holmes' arrangements for the following day.

As we sat and talked, I was suddenly struck by the change in my friend's demeanor. He was no longer anxious; rather, he was the picture of equanimity as he sat there smoking his pipe and sipping his brandy. Although I tried on several occasions to draw Holmes out, he refused to be baited. Rather, he looked at me and repeated a maxim that I had heard on any number of occasions, "You have seen but you do not observe.

"Admittedly, I have a slight advantage in that I was able to examine Langlois' flat without interference.

Still, the fact remains that I have transmitted to you all the salient facts in an unvarnished manner. If you have any questions, I shall be more than happy to answer them; otherwise, I will bid you good night and see you for breakfast at 8 o'clock."

Holmes looked at me expectantly, but try as I might, I was unable to devise any questions for my friend. After a short but uncomfortable pause, I said, "Good night, Holmes."

When I made my way to breakfast the next morning, I found my friend waiting for me. "I took the liberty of asking Mrs. Hudson to prepare coffee, eggs and a rasher of bacon for you. It should be here momentarily."

He then returned to the paper he had been reading. "Anything interesting?" I inquired.

"The Times has a small story about the arrival of Theophile Declasse, the French statesman, who is staying at the Savoy. Fortunately, he has led the reporter to believe that he is simply here on holiday."

"It appears as though you were correct about where Mycroft would ensconce the various delegations."

"Half right, at least," replied Holmes. "There is nothing here about the Russian representative."

My breakfast arrived and as I was eating, I saw Holmes glance at his watch on three occasions. Finally, my friend exclaimed, "Do hurry, Watson. It is nearly half past the hour, and we must make certain we arrive at St. Paul's on time."

After we had descended the stairs and hailed a cab, I turned to Holmes and said, "May I ask what is so special about this meeting at St. Paul's."

Holmes merely looked at me in an uncomprehending manner and then he replied, "Surely you jest," before he lapsed into silence.

The tallest structure in London, St. Paul's Cathedral is certainly one of the most beautiful houses of worship in England and perhaps all of Europe. I will not bore readers here with the storied history of the building, although if truth be told, I was rather excited to be visiting it. Like so many Londoners, I confess to having taken this masterwork for granted. Once as a youngster, I had been taken inside, but I had not returned since.

Aside from the fact that it had been designed by Sir Christopher Wren to replace the previous cathedral which had been destroyed in the Great Fire of London, I knew little else about the building except that both the Duke of Wellington and Admiral Horatio Nelson, as well as Wren himself, had been interred there.

After climbing Ludgate Hill and proceeding along the road that abutted the cathedral, albeit a short distance away, the cab deposited us closest to the South Transept entrance. As we walked towards the magnificent structure, all I could do was admire the beauty of the stunning building and wonder about the views that the upper galleries must afford.

After entering, I whispered to Holmes, "Where exactly are we going?"

He pointed up to the first level and said, "The Whispering Gallery."

"The Whispering Gallery? What is that?"

"You will soon find out, old friend," he replied, and I thought I heard him chuckle.

We entered a staircase and began our ascent. After several flights my leg began to throb as my old wound reminded me of my age – and my past. I said to Holmes, "How many steps are there?"

"To the Whispering Gallery or in total?"

"To where we are going," I said with a tinge of exasperation in my voice.

"There are 259 steps to the Whispering Gallery, of which you have climbed 148. You have but 111 left." When Holmes said that I felt a definite twinge in my leg. "Should you wish to continue after we have concluded our business there, you have another 117 steps to the Stone Gallery, at which point you can walk outside around the dome, and, if you are still so inclined, just 166 additional steps will bring you to the Golden Gallery. Again, you may walk outside and enjoy unparalleled views of London. I highly recommend it."

By this time, I knew I was nearing the end of my trek. When we reached the landing, I entered the gallery and slumped down on the bench seat that seemed to encompass the entire dome with an occasional niche that I assumed harbored a door that led somewhere else in the cathedral.

"Wait here, Watson. Keep an eye on all who enter. I am going to sit directly across from you."

"To what end?" I said, but Holmes either had not heard me, or he had decided to ignore me. Taking stock of my surroundings, I noticed that there were but two other people besides Holmes and myself in the gallery.

Suddenly, a large group of tourists, perhaps twenty-five or thirty people, entered the gallery from the doorway to my left. I could make out the voice of the man serving as their guide as he began to discuss the artwork that adorned the dome. Learning that they were eight scenes from the life of St. Paul, painted by Sir James Thornhill, I found myself listening to the docent as well as snatches of their various conversations when all of a sudden, I thought I heard a whispering voice say quite distinctly, "This is your last warning, Mr. Holmes." To say I was startled would be an understatement. I looked across and could tell immediately that something had spurred Holmes into action.

Suddenly, I heard the spectral voice a second time, "Remember, Mycroft's life hangs in the balance."

When I looked over at Holmes, I saw that he had disappeared. Turning my attention back to the tourists who were now leaving, I could tell that one or two of them must have heard the voice as well. A minute or two later, Holmes was standing by my side, "Did you see who said it?"

"No," I said. "The only people here besides you and me are those two, the tourists and their docent."

"Docent? There are no docents yet. The first guided tour is not scheduled to begin until 10 a.m."

"Well, there was a man talking about the art in the gallery, and I just assumed he was a guide employed by the cathedral."

"Did you get a good look at him?"

"Not very, I'm afraid. There were tourists blocking my view. However, he appeared to be rather tall and thin. I believe he had a beard, and he had a most distinctive voice."

"Oh, Watson. I fear I may have gravely underestimated our foe."

"Why do you say that?"

"You will recall that it was I who arranged the meeting here. I was hoping to use the rather unusual acoustics of the Whispering Gallery to my advantage and take him by surprise. But he has turned the tables on me and delivered one final warning. With the conference scheduled to begin tomorrow, I am afraid we are running out of time."

"Holmes can you explain how we, as well as a few of the tourists, heard that voice, even though it was a whisper and we were quite far apart?"

Holmes chuckled and then said, "People have known about the strange quirk in this gallery almost since the church was built, but it was only in the 1870s that Lord Rayleigh discovered that sound waves actually 'creep horizontally,' to use his words, around the dome, through a process of reflection."

Having warmed to his subject, Holmes then delivered a treatise as we descended the stairs. Seeing that it distracted him for a few minutes, I indulged him, interrupting now and again to ask a question, the answer to which interested me not in the least. At one point, Holmes even suggested I read *The Theory of Sound,* which he described as Rayleigh's magnum opus on the subject. "While there is a great deal of useful information in the first volume, I found the second volume even more illuminating. I have copies of both that you may borrow at any time."

I promised to put them at the top of the list of books I planned to read – a promise I had no intention of keeping.

He continued musing about the properties of sound all the way through our cab ride to Baker Street. However, as we exited the cab, I said to Holmes, "I know you are worried about your brother, my friend, and you can count on me to do anything you might ask to save Mycroft's life."

At that Holmes stood stock still, his hand on the knob to our front door. After about five seconds, he turned slowly to me and said simply, "Thank you, old friend."

I could tell there was more to his expression of gratitude, but he had already dashed up the stairs as I was turning over what had just occurred in my mind.

Chapter 14

I followed Holmes up the stairs and when I entered our rooms, I found him pulling one of his indexes from the shelf. Before I could say anything, he began upbraiding himself. "I have been an idiot, Watson. For all your prattling about my supposed deductive ability, I have failed myself in a most sublime display of obstinacy.

"Here I was priding myself on being one step ahead of our opponent when in fact he has been two – perhaps three – steps ahead of me the entire time. How could I not have foreseen this?"

"Foreseen what?" I asked, totally bewildered by the sudden change in my old friend's manner.

Ignoring my question, he continued on in that same vein, "But now that I have come to a full realization of what they have done, I can take the appropriate steps to rescue my brother and to end this attempt to scuttle the peace conference he had planned."

"How on Earth do you plan to do that?"

"It is actually quite simple. I just need to make a few more inquiries. After all, having missed the mark so badly, I wouldn't want my future efforts to go wide of the target as well."

"Is there anything I can do to help?"

"Indeed, old friend." Reaching down, he lifted a small parcel that had been newly wrapped in butcher paper. Handing it to me, he said, "I wonder if you would so kind as to place this in your physician's bag and see that it arrives safely with this note in the hands of Dr. Smith."

"That's not the *Cotton Vitellius A XV* manuscript, is it?"

"Watson, you amaze me. I am capable of accomplishing a great many things, but making a stolen medieval manuscript appear in my room is not one of them. No, old friend, this is something I picked up that I hoped would cheer up Dr. Smith. After you have delivered it, I want you to gather up Lestrade, and we shall all meet back here at four."

I tucked the parcel away in my bag and descended the stairs. I wondered if this weren't some ploy of

Holmes to get me out of the way for a while, but I decided that was a rather silly notion.

Obviously, things were coming to a head, but I still found myself anxious. My friend had been involved in any number of cases whose resolution had been a matter of life and death. However, I could not recall a single instance where so many lives might depend upon the outcome of his exertions.

When I arrived at the museum, I was informed Dr. Smith was attending a conference at the recently chartered University of Leeds and was not expected to return for a day or two. I was uncertain of what to do with my parcel. I considered leaving it in Smith's office, but since Holmes had used the word "safely," I decided to keep it in my bag and inform Holmes about the academic's absence.

Next, I hailed a hansom and headed for Lambeth. As my cab crossed over the Lambeth Bridge, I was thinking back on our long association with Lestrade. A few minutes later, I was knocking on the door of a small cottage on Whitgift Street where the Inspector lived. At my second knock, I heard him bellow, "Just a minute! Just a minute!"

Upon opening the door, he smiled and said, "Well isn't this a surprise, Dr. Watson. To what do I owe the honor?"

"Holmes asked me to gather you and for the both of us to meet him back at Baker Street at three."

"It sounds as though he may be onto something," observed Lestrade.

Although I was inclined to agree with the Inspector, I said nothing.

"Imagine Mr. Sherlock Holmes requesting my assistance *two* days in a row," he continued.

Despite Lestrade's continual prodding and poking all the way back to Baker Street, I was determined to say nothing unless I had cleared it with Holmes first.

As soon as we had entered the house, I could tell that something unusual was taking place. Mrs. Hudson came hurrying down the stairs all aflutter and, without stopping to greet us, continued into the kitchen, saying over her shoulder, "Thank goodness, you are finally here. He has been waiting for you."

I looked at Lestrade and said, "That is most unlike her. I wonder what the deuce is going on." My question was soon answered as I opened the door and saw Holmes chatting with another man, whose back was to us. When he turned, I must admit to being taken aback. Standing in front of me was Sir Henry Campbell-Bannerman, First Lord of the Treasury, who had accepted the post less than two years earlier from King Edward VII. Although a few inches shorter than Holmes and more broad-shouldered than either of us, the man who was the first to use the title "Prime Minister," which had only been officially given recognition when it was added to the order of precedence in 1905, was a commanding figure with piercing light eyes and a moustache that might have been the envy of any who favored such facial accoutrements.

"Watson, Lestrade, allow me to introduce Sir Henry Campbell-Bannerman."

To say I was taken aback would not even begin to capture my feelings. Although we had entertained visitors of all stripes, including royalty, at Baker Street, meeting the leader of one's country remains a slightly off-putting experience.

The Prime Minister turned to me and said, "At long last, I have wanted to meet you for some time so that I could tell you how much I have enjoyed your literary efforts. I had often thought to write you, but …"

As his words trailed off, I jumped in, saying "Completely understandable, Prime Minister. After all, you have a great many more important things to occupy your time."

After Holmes had introduced Lestrade, the Prime Minister grasped the Inspector's hand and shook it warmly. "Mr. Holmes has told me of your many years of devoted service at Scotland Yard. He also informs me that you are, at present, in a bit of a bind. Fear not, Inspector, I promise you we will sort everything out."

"If you don't mind my saying so, sir. It's not sorting out that I want nor need. I just wish to have my good name restored."

"And so it shall be, Lestrade. I promised you we would clear you name and erase the stain on your reputation and so we shall," said Holmes.

At that point Mrs. Hudson entered with tea and biscuits. After she had deposited the tray, she attempted to linger for a bit, but Holmes deftly escorted her to the door. We then adjoined to the table. After pouring the tea for everyone, Holmes said, "Gentlemen, we have some serious business in front of us tonight."

"So I was given to understand from your letter, Mr. Holmes. May I inquire as to what part I am to play in your little production this evening?" asked the Prime Minister.

Holmes then proceeded to explain in painstaking detail the role he expected each of us to carry out that evening. When he had finished, he smiled, refilled his pipe, and after he had managed a good draw, he looked at us and said, "Any questions?"

"Blimey, Mr. Holmes," exclaimed Lestrade, apparently forgetting the Prime Minister was sitting fewer than two feet to his left.

"There are no guarantees," replied my friend, "but I would like to think this plan has a greater chance of success than the several others I have devised."

"I must say, Mr. Holmes," interjected the Prime Minister, "you do make it all sound rather simple. Do you think such a basic stratagem will succeed?"

"I think, Your Excellency, this plan may well succeed because it is so…," and then he paused as if searching for just the right word. Finally, he turned to me with a mischievous grin and said, "so … elementary."

I had to chuckle, but Holmes continued undeterred. "Now, before we adjourn, let us review the timing – and I cannot stress enough – how important it is that that each of you hit your mark at just the right moment."

Holmes then quizzed each of us in turn about our assignments and the precise moment when each of us was to arrive and utter our lines. When we had finished, Holmes thanked us and stressed, "What we do this evening may well determine how badly England, perhaps all of Europe, is buffeted by the winds of war in the near future."

With that reminder, he bid Lestrade and the Prime Minister good day and said he would see them at the appointed hour.

We had a few hours before the curtain was to rise on Holmes' production. As we sat there, discussing the case and the myriad problems it had presented, the time passed quickly. It was just a quarter after five when I thought I discerned a faint knock on the front door downstairs. Sure enough, a few minutes later Mrs. Hudson knocked on our door. After Holmes bade her enter, she said, "A gentleman to see you sir, He would not give his name, but he did instruct me to tell you that it was a matter of the utmost urgency."

"Show him up," replied Holmes, and a minute later Alexander Dennison entered our rooms. Holmes rose and greeted him, "Mr. Dennison, what brings you to my humble abode?"

"As I am sure you are aware, Mr. Holmes, no one has seen your brother for the past two days."

"Really?" replied Holmes. "We speak but occasionally, although now that you mention it, I have not heard from my brother in quite some time."

"I do not know if you are aware of this, and I hope that I am not telling tales out of school, but we have a most important conference that is scheduled to get underway tomorrow."

"I believe I have heard some vague mention of it," replied my friend. "Important, you say?"

"Indeed," said Dennison, "and as you might expect, your brother was to lead our delegation."

"And you say he is missing?" asked Holmes.

"Indeed, sir," replied the young man. "Moreover, Geoffrey Langlois, one of my co-workers also seems to have disappeared."

"Well, I can assure you that Mycroft is quite capable of looking after himself. As for Mr. Langlois, I am at a loss for words."

"I am sure you are right about your brother, but who is to lead us in the conference? What are our positions to be on the various issues which are certain to arise? It promises to be quite a thorny affair, Mr. Holmes. And while my comrades and I can fend for ourselves in our particular areas of expertise, things would obviously proceed in a more orderly fashion were your brother present."

"And the conference begins tomorrow, you say?"

"Yes sir. We have an opening reception tomorrow night at eight at the Cavendish. Your brother had persuaded Rosa Lewis to prepare the meal."

"Ha! Of course he would," laughed Holmes."

"Sir, I do not think I am impressing upon you the gravity of the situation."

"I have little interest in politics," said Holmes. "Still, I shall make some discreet inquiries as the whereabouts of both my brother and Mr. Langlois, and I shall contact you tomorrow afternoon should I learn anything."

"Thank you, Mr. Holmes," he said. Turning to me, he nodded and said, "Then I shall wish both of you a good evening, and I look forward to hearing from you tomorrow." He then proceeded down the stairs and I heard the door close.

Striding to the window, I watched him walk down Baker Street before I turned to Holmes and said, "Well, that was a rather unexpected caller."

"Not entirely," replied my friend. "I had rather thought that one of Mycroft's minions might contact us regarding his sudden disappearance."

"Well, that's certainly quite possible," I replied, "but why did you lie to the man? You have been searching for Mycroft ever since you received word of his abduction. Moreover, you will see that man in just a few hours – or had you forgot?"

At that Holmes chuckled. "You know I have not forgot, but every now and again, I find that a bit of mendacity will serve my ends far better than a healthy helping of the truth."

"Do you suspect him?"

"Until Mycroft is once again sitting in his office or his chair at the Diogenes, everyone – with a few notable exceptions, of course – is a suspect."

"I do hope I fit among the 'notable exceptions,'" I said.

"That is beneath you, Watson. Now, I must step out for a bit as I have a few more things to which I must attend. I shall return as quickly as possible. Then we can enjoy the sumptuous repast Mrs. Hudson is preparing, and following that, with a bit of luck and a great deal of planning, we can close the books on this sordid affair."

"I have never known you to depend on luck," I replied.

"Watson, you wound me. Luck has no place in the rational world. I was merely playing off the words of the American statesman, Benjamin Franklin, who once observed, 'Diligence is the mother of good luck.'"

And with that, he was out the door. Although there are times when I find myself fully prepared to engage with Holmes – and on some few occasions, I have given as well I have received – when he cites Benjamin Franklin, I am more than willing to concede the point.

Chapter 15

It was just about half past six, when I thought I detected Holmes' tread on the stairs. Looking at my watch, I realized he had been gone less than an hour. A few seconds later, he entered the sitting room. After hanging up his coat and hat, he turned and asked, "Have there been any messages for me?"

"Not that I know of. I don't recall hearing the bell ring either, although you may check with Mrs. Hudson if you like."

"No, no. I am certain she would have shared any communiqués with you."

"Something important? I asked.

"Just some information I had hoped to ascertain, in the event that it should come into play this evening."

"Holmes, I do hope you realize the enormous stakes involved. This is quite unlike any of our other adventures. They have attempted to distract you by throwing multiple cases in your way all the while carrying out a most diabolical scheme – but to what end?"

"To make certain that Mycroft would be unable to oversee the peace conference and to hamper my efforts to locate my brother. We are dealing here with highly trained professionals. Men – and perhaps women, as well – whose first allegiance is to their country, and if their interests happen to conflict with England's, well then so much the worse for His Majesty."

Just at that moment, I heard the bell ring, and a few seconds later I detected the patter of young feet ascending the stairs. That was followed by a full-fledged knock on our door and a young voice bellowing, "Mr. 'Olmes! Mr. 'Olmes!"

My friend raced to the door and threw it open. Standing there was a lad of no more than eight or nine who was desperately trying to catch his breath. Holding out a note, he said, "Mr. Wiggins said to get this to you as soon as possible, so I run all the way."

Holmes took the note and read it. He looked at the youngster and said, "You have done incredibly well! And you ran all the way you said?"

"Yes sir, Mr. 'Olmes"

My friend then gave the boy some coins and said, "Go downstairs and tell Mrs. Hudson that I said she is to give you my dinner."

The child's eyes had grown large when Holmes had handed him the coins, and they now grew larger still – if that were possible.

Turning to me, Holmes said, "Watson, I shall do my best to be there at eight, but if I am delayed, tell Sir Henry that he must hold down the fort until my arrival. Assure him that reinforcements are on the way."

With that he donned his coat and hat and was out the door. I was so taken aback that I found myself speechless. It was only after he had departed that I spied the note the boy had delivered sitting on the table. Holmes must have placed it there while putting on his coat and forgot to retrieve it. Wondering what vital piece of information it might contain, I picked it up and there in the scrawl that I had come to recognize as Wiggins' handwriting, I saw only the word: "Hackney."

As I bolted down a solitary dinner, so conscious was I of the time, the one-word message for Holmes kept reverberating in my mind. Hackney, I knew, had several possible definitions. It was the name of a borough in London and a theatre therein, as well as a village in Derbyshire near Matlock and a town in Australia. I believed I had also read at one point of a Hackney in the United States, perhaps in Kansas or Missouri. Complicating matters further, Hackney was also a breed of horse and pony as well the name for a common type of horse-drawn carriage. Despite my best efforts, I could not see through the veil that hid the word's significance as Holmes apparently had.

So finally at about a quarter to eight, I donned my coat and, since it was quite a pleasant evening, I set out on foot for Mycroft's office in Whitehall. I was really rather hoping Holmes would not be late as I had no idea how long Sir Henry and I would be able to stall should my friend prove tardy in the extreme.

As I entered the building that housed Mycroft's office, I confess that I had no idea what I was going to say or do. The porter showed me to Mycroft's office and there I found Diedrich Bern, Deniz Cenk and Alexander Dennison occupying the same seats they had on my earlier visit. While Geoffrey Langlois' seat was conspicuously empty, the chair at the head of the table, where Mycroft would normally sit, had been filled by Sir Henry Campbell-Bannerman.

Rising, he greeted me, "Ah, Doctor Watson, right on time." Looking about, he then noticed that I was alone. Before he could say anything, I said, "A word, Sir Henry, if you please."

We then walked to the far side of the room where I informed him in hushed tones of Holmes' sudden departure from Baker Street and his parting instructions to me.

"Between the two of us, I think we can manage to keep these young men at bay for some time, don't you?"

He then strode to the other side of the room and, after motioning me to a chair at the table, began to speak. "Gentlemen, I know you are familiar with Dr. Watson and I have asked him to join us because he brings a unique perspective on foreign affairs, having served in Afghanistan as well as having advised Mr. Sherlock Holmes on any number of matters involving the heads of foreign states – all of which required a great deal of tact and diplomacy."

"Will Mister Holmes be joining us as well?" asked Bern.

"He is expected," I replied, "although he is quite preoccupied on another case and his attendance this evening might best be described as uncertain."

"With all due respect, Sir Henry," said Dennison, "this conference is now about securing alliances and planning for the worst in the event Europe should suddenly disintegrate into war. While I certainly respect Dr. Watson and Mister Holmes, I would have to question their supposed 'perspective' on foreign affairs, especially as it relates to present circumstances, which you claim they possesses."

"Would you care to elaborate?" replied the Prime Minister.

"We need someone with the unique breadth of knowledge that Mycroft Holmes possesses. While peace remains our primary objective, should conflict break out, we must have plans in place for deploying our army and navy, for reinforcing our troops, not to mention setting up supply lines and field hospitals."

"Well put Mr. Dennison. Have you anything to add Mr. Bern or Mr. Cenk?"

After pausing to gather his thoughts, Bern began to speak, "I agree with my colleague that we need the seeming omniscience which Mycroft Holmes appears to bring to bear on such matters. In his absence, I believe we have but one option: We must postpone the conference until Mr. Holmes has been located."

"I fear that would make us look weak to our allies," interjected Cenk. "We call for a top-secret conference, put everything into play and then suddenly cancel the conference the day it is to begin. I can only imagine the conversations between the French emissaries as they return to Paris, and I fear those would pale in comparison to what the Russians might be thinking. No, Prime Minister, somehow, some way, we must get through this conference, and hopefully when he returns, Mr. Holmes will be able to rectify any mistakes that we might make."

"I would second that opinion," offered Dennison.

The four of them kept the debate going for another hour at least, and I thought Sir Henry was doing an admirable job of buying time.

Eventually, the Prime Minister decided that Bern – given his intimate knowledge of the German Empire – would act as an interim lead negotiator, barring the sudden reappearance of Mycroft. The resolution did not appear to sit well with Dennison; nevertheless, he remained silent, keeping whatever misgivings he might harbor to himself.

Shortly before nine, I excused myself and stepped outside to tell Lestrade his presence would not be required unless Holmes made an appearance.'

"Whatever you say, Doctor," he replied.

I returned to find that they had taken a short break. While we were enjoying a cup of coffee, Sir Henry pulled me aside, "I know you said to stall, Watson, but where the deuce is Holmes? We have been at this for well over an hour. I don't see how I can protract this discussion for much longer."

When we returned to the table, they began to address the agenda for the conference. The reception was to take place the following night and the first official meeting was to convene at 9 a.m. the day after that in the Marble Arch.

After we had gone over all the particulars two more times, Sir Henry looked at me, and when I shrugged, he said, "Gentlemen, it is drawing late. I shall see you tomorrow night at eight, prior to the reception."

After Bern, Cenk and Dennison had departed, Sir Henry said, "Unless he has been gravely injured, I fear your Mister Holmes has some explaining to do."

"I shall convey your message to him when I see him," I promised.

After apologizing to Lestrade, who had remained outside, and telling him I would be in touch, I took a cab to Baker Street and when I alighted, I saw that our rooms were in almost total darkness. Since it was not yet 10 p.m., I rather doubted Holmes had gone to bed. And truth be told, although my friend was often totally unpredictable in his ways, I must confess that I was beginning to worry.

As I entered the sitting room, I saw that the fire had died down, but the embers were still giving off a soft glow. I was just about to turn on the lights when I heard Holmes' voice say, "Please Watson, if you don't mind, I would much prefer a darkened room right now. I find the absence of all distractions, including light, both soothing and invigorating."

"Holmes, I believe you have some explaining to do, and I also think that you owe Sir Henry an apology."

"Yes, yes. I am certain that you are correct on both counts, but my absence from that meeting was unavoidable. In fact, I might even go so far as to say that it was imperative that I not be in attendance."

"Nevertheless, you were the one who promised Sir Henry you would be there. You were the one who instructed me to have Sir Henry stall until you arrived, and now I return home to find you sitting in a darkened room. I have no idea how long you have been here, but judging by the aroma of tobacco, I would hazard a guess that you have been sitting here for at least two pipes – possibly three."

"You outdo yourself, Watson. Yes, I have just finished my second pipe. And you are quite correct, I do owe you an explanation and Sir Henry an apology but now is not the time for either."

"But Holmes ..."

He cut me off before I could offer any further protest. "I know it is difficult, Watson. And I am well aware of how things must appear. Unfortunately, all I can do at present is to ask your continued forgiveness and to beg your further indulgence."

While Holmes and I had been friends for decades, I must admit I found it hard to accept his apology without any hint of an explanation. Thinking I might feel differently in the morning, I replied, "If that is the way it must be, then so be it." Heading towards my bedroom, I said simply, "Good night, Holmes."

To this day, I cannot swear whether I actually heard it or my overwrought imagination simply wanted to hear it, but I thought I heard Holmes utter the words, "Good night, old friend," followed by, "I would not burden you with any more of this."

I thought about asking Holmes if he had spoken and then decided against it. Had he wanted me to hear his remark, he would have said it in such a way that I would not question my own sanity.

Feeling totally agitated and adrift on a sea of wild speculation, I found sleep difficult to come by that night.

Chapter 16

I awoke the next morning still wondering whether Holmes had actually spoken to me or whether the words had been a wishful figment of my imagination.

As I dressed, I decided that I would confront him and pose my question, but I soon learned from Mrs. Hudson that my friend had risen early, taken only a cup of coffee for breakfast – "That man," she muttered – and departed Baker Street without giving our landlady any idea of where he was going or when he might return.

"However, he did ask that I give you this," she said, pulling an envelope from her apron pocket. "He sealed it," she said matter-of-factly but with just the slightest twinge of annoyance in her voice. "I can only assume it must be quite important."

After she had placed it on the table, she waited expectantly. "I will read it after I have finished my breakfast," I said. "Thank you, Mrs. Hudson."

No sooner had she left then I tore open the envelope and there in my friend's spidery hand was a short note:

My dear Watson,

*Again my apologies for my absence
last night and any consternation it might
have caused you. Believe me when I say,
had I been able to make you aware of my
plans, I would have. If you are so
inclined, please don your most
disreputable clothes and meet me at the
circular junction on Dockside Road at
noon.*

As always, your faithful servant,

S.H.

PS Your ears do not deceive you

I must admit I was taken aback, not only by the
note itself but also by Holmes' unexpected display of
candor. Looking at my watch, I determined that I had
plenty of time in which to finish breakfast, adjust my
attire and make my way to the Thames.

While Holmes has always relished those cases in
which he could don a disguise, I must confess I could
never see the appeal. I am certain part of my reticence
stems from the fact that I am not the natural performer
that Holmes is. When he assumes a character, he quite

literally becomes that individual. I, on the other hand, have always felt far more comfortable in my own skin.

And so, despite my misgivings, I removed my collar, tie and other garments and donned the wretched garb provided by Holmes which I had worn to the docks on our previous visit. Feeling rather foolish, I left through the rear of Baker Street, as per Mrs. Hudson's instructions, and managed to find a dogcart willing to take me to the river.

As I alighted from the cab on Dockside Road, I was immediately struck anew by the smell that emanated from the river. Taking my disheveled appearance into account as I surveyed those around me, I decided that I had done a reasonably good job with my disguise although I was certain Holmes would find fault with something.

As I neared the circular junction, I saw Holmes approaching from the direction of the docks. I was able to recognize him only because he too was wearing the same attire, including that singular hat, he had donned for our previous visit.

From a distance, I could see him taking the measure of my appearance and when we finally met, he smiled and said, "Watson, I do believe you have outdone yourself." I smiled at his compliment but he soon corrected himself, saying, "I should have told you not to shave but this opportunity arose rather unexpectedly. Perhaps you can affect a limp as we go along. Such an affliction will also make you less liable to be hired."

"Holmes, exactly what are we doing here, and why is my presence required?"

"I find it necessary to investigate another building. I finally learned that the warehouse where the smugglers were supposedly operating had been leased by one Alexander Dennison."

"My word, isn't that…"

"Yes, it's the name of one of Mycroft's assistants."

"So, he must be the one behind the whole plot!"

"Have you forgotten who signed for the desk and who allegedly ordered the safe? No, a name on a lease means nothing. However, during my research I also discovered a second warehouse, quite close to the one I examined, had been leased to a Deniz Cenk."

"Another of Mycroft's assistants," I exclaimed. "Holmes, what does it all mean?"

"That is precisely what we are here to ascertain. Do you see that red building up on the left? That is the warehouse I wish to examine."

"And you want me to serve as your lookout once again?"

"If you would be so kind."

When we arrived at the building, Holmes knocked on the front door. "Let us see if we can enter legally and perhaps earn a day's wages."

As Holmes knocked on the door a second time, a passing laborer yelled, "There's no work there. That place is deserted."

Smiling at me, Holmes said, "I will be as quick as possible. If you see someone coming bang on the door and yell, 'Mr. Margate, are you in there?'"

He then disappeared around the side of the building. I kept my solitary vigil hoping it would soon be over. Perhaps twenty minutes later, Holmes reappeared from around the side of the building. It was impossible to read the expression on his face, and although it was difficult, I refrained from asking questions until we had left the docks behind us and were nearing the circular junction.

Finally, I could restrain myself no longer, "Well, did you discover anything useful."

"It was most productive but equally infuriating."

"How so?"

"I know that Mycroft was there for at least several hours."

"Pray tell, how did you arrive at that conclusion? Did he leave you a note?"

"Not exactly," he replied smiling. "You see, when Mycroft and I were youngsters, we would play our own version of 'Sardines.' You are familiar with the game, Watson?"

"I am. One child hides and all the others try to find him. As each child discovers him, they join him in his hiding place. Used to play it myself as a lad."

"Yes, well, since there were but two of us and since Mycroft was sedentary, even as a young man, we devised our own game, which we called 'Impressions.' I would walk through all the rooms in our home, committing them to memory. Then, while I wasn't looking, Mycroft would add something or alter something in one room in a subtly obvious way. I would then revisit the rooms trying to ascertain the change. And we would take turns doing this, so on the next round Mycroft then had to determine which room I had been in and what had been altered."

"That's all well and good," I replied, "but what has it to do with Mycroft being in the warehouse?"

"We had a terrible row one day because no matter how many times I considered the rooms, I could not discover what had been changed. Finally, Mycroft admitted that he had carved his initials on the underside of a windowsill."

"I insisted it wasn't fair, while he maintained that I should have examined things more closely."

"And?"

"While I was examining the warehouse, I discovered the letters 'MH' carved into the underside of a sill. For some reason, they were inverted as HM, but those are Mycroft's initials."

"My word, Holmes. That is extraordinary."

"Not really, Watson. The warehouse was completely empty save for a bench, an old blanket and a bucket."

"So there were no other clues? No hints as to where Mycroft might be?"

"I didn't say that. There were four other symbols carved into the wood – one number and three letters. Taken together they read 5 M-E-N."

"What on Earth does that mean? Do you think Mycroft was abducted by five men?"

"No, with Mycroft, things are never quite what they seem. Besides 'five men' in and of itself, tells us nothing. No, I can only surmise that Mycroft was trying to tell me who had kidnapped him or perhaps he learned where they intended to take him next. At any rate until we are able to ascertain the meaning of '5 MEN,' we can proceed no further."

At that moment, we heard the three blasts of a ship steaming up the Thames. "I wonder if that is the Black Prince," I said. "I read the ship would be stopping here before setting out for the Mediterranean."

"We have time for neither ships nor speculation," replied Holmes. "The reception begins at 8 this evening, and the conference formally convenes tomorrow morning at 9. We have fewer than 24 hours in which to find and free Mycroft. And I have a great deal of research to do regarding the streets of London.

Chapter 17

When we returned to Baker Street, Holmes quickly washed up and changed his clothing. Eschewing lunch, he began pulling various reference books from the shelves and at one point, he ventured into the lumber room and returned with several more tomes.

I watched as my friend ransacked his way through any number of volumes, stopping occasionally to jot something down on a sheet of foolscap. After more than an hour, he looked at me and said, "This might not be as difficult as I had imagined. There are only six streets in London that begin with the letters 'M-E-N.'"

He then read them off to me: Mendip Close, Mendip Road, Mendora Road, Menelik Road, Mentmore Close and Mentmore Terrace.

"Of those the two most likely are Mendip Close and Mendip Road. Both are on the other side of the Thames. The other four are all quite public, so to speak, located as they are near cricket pitches, schools, shops and the like. No, Watson. I believe we are getting close.

"Come my friend, we have a fair amount of ground to cover and not much time."

And so before long we were crossing Albert Bridge and heading for Battersea. The area was home to a number of large firms, including the Morgan Crucible Company, and I thought this would make an excellent place to conceal any kidnapping victim. However, when we arrived at Mendip Road, we discovered a family with several small children residing in Number 5. Perhaps an hour or so later, we arrived at Mendip Close only to learn that much of the block had been demolished and that Number 5 no longer existed.

Although Holmes had remained his impassive self throughout the entire journey, I thought I detected some frustration as we began our journey back to Baker Street.

Trying to console my friend, I remarked, "Well, this afternoon appears to have been a journey of twists and turns but to no avail. However, we still have some time left."

Although I thought he hadn't heard me, so deep in contemplation did he seem, I was dumbstruck when he suddenly sat bolt upright, and said, "Watson, would you be so kind as to repeat your last remark?"

After thinking for a second, I said, "However, we still have time left."

"No, no. The one before that!" His face had grown slightly flushed, so I considered my words carefully before I finally said, "This afternoon appears to have been a journey of twists and turns but…"

He stopped me. "Not a journey of twists and turns, Watson, but 'a man of twists of turns.' How could I have missed it!?! It was so painfully obvious." He then leaned out the window and yelled to the driver to stop.

The cab halted quite near Kennington Park, and Holmes jumped out, "Watson, you need to collect Lestrade at once and bring him to Baker Street. You are not too terribly far from his home.

"I am going to hire a cab and see if my suspicions are correct. If they are, I shall contact you at Baker Street as soon as possible. Oh, Watson, tell Lestrade, he might want to bring some darbies, and since he is still suspended, you might suggest he bring his Webley as well."

With that, Holmes set off on foot down Brixton Road, mumbling to himself. I thought I detected him saying, "Almost an error of epic proportions."

Fortunately, Lestrade was home and when I relayed Holmes' requests to him, he was more than willing to oblige. As we drove to Baker Street, he said,

"You know, Doctor, I enjoyed having a few days off, but truth be told I cannot wait to return to duty."

"Well, that may be fairly soon, I think, but I am making no promises."

Upon our arrival, we had little to do but sit and wait to hear from Holmes. As we passed the time, with an occasional awkward silence, in lieu of conversation, Mrs. Hudson arrived with a tray of sandwiches and coffee. "Knowing your rather unorthodox hours, you may not eat again for quite some time."

After she had left, both Lestrade and I feasted on her largess as we began to reminisce about a number of the many cases we had worked on together.

The sun was just beginning to set when I heard the bell ring. A few seconds later a pair of young legs scurried up the stairs and the knocking – or should I say pounding – on the door commenced.

Opening it, I discovered one of Holmes' street urchins holding a note. "This is for you Doctor Watson, from Mister 'Olmes." I thanked the lad and pressed a few coins into his hand.

After he had departed, I opened the paper and immediately recognized Holmes' rather distinctive hand.

"What does it say?" Lestrade asked.

Watson,

> *If you and Inspector Lestrade*
> *would be so kind as to meet*
> *me at Cloister Walk and St.*
> *Katharine's Way at precisely*
> *9 p.m., I shall be eternally in*
> *your debt. Both of you should*
> *wear dark clothing and arm*
> *yourselves. A dark lantern*
> *might also prove useful.*
> *Finally, bring two or three*
> *sandwiches in a basket.*

> > *Sincerely,*

> > *S.H.*

"He certainly doesn't give much away, does he?" remarked Lestrade.

"You know Holmes has always been rather close-mouthed."

"Indeed I do," laughed the Inspector.

Glancing at my watch, I saw that it was slightly past the half hour. I said to Lestrade, "If we leave here at 8, we should arrive in plenty of time. You are wearing navy, which should be fine. I'm just going to change into a black coat."

After one more cigarette, we descended the stairs, hailed a cab and perhaps three-quarters of an hour later, we alighted at the designated intersection. A few minutes later, Holmes approached us in disguise. Again, I recognized him only because I had seen him wearing the jacket on another occasion. The bushy brown beard was, however, a new touch.

Sidling up to Lestrade, Holmes said in a rather broad brogue, "Spare a few coppers for an old navvy down on his luck?"

"Off with you now and be quick about it, or I'll run in you in," replied Lestrade.

"And I was told you had no legal standing," replied Holmes in his normal voice.

"Ah, Mr. Holmes, I rather suspected it was you all along," replied Lestrade.

While I was inclined to doubt the veracity of Lestrade's statement, Holmes appeared to give him the benefit of the doubt.

"An excellent observation, Lestrade," said my friend. "I have located the ship where I believe Mycroft is being held. There is one ruffian at the base of the gangplank, and at least one more on board below decks. I have been watching it for the past two hours, and those are the only souls I have seen near the vessel.

"She is berthed about three-quarters of a mile from here, at the very end of the wharf. Here is what I propose we do." Holmes then outlined his plan, and so it was that some thirty minutes later Lestrade, carrying the food, started out along the wharf, whistling a merry tune as he went.

Holmes and I kept to the shadows on the other side, hiding behind barrels and crates. I should guess we remained a good fifty feet from Lestrade.

As he approached the sentinel, the man began to eye Lestrade. When the inspector was still some forty feet away, the guard said, "This is private property. You're not allowed to be here."

"I've brought you and your mate food and drink," replied Lestrade, who held up the basket as he continued his leisurely pace towards the guard.

"I don't know anything about that," said the man in a voice that radiated suspicion.

"If you don't want it, I'll eat it meself," said Lestrade.

"I never said I didn't want it. What's in the basket?"

"Chicken sandwiches, ham sandwiches and some scones."

"Leave it there and get on your way," said the guard.

Putting the basket down, Lestrade pushed it towards the guard and said, "Just let me fix my shoe. I think there's a pebble in it."

With that Lestrade sat down and removed his shoe.

Believing Lestrade helpless, the guard stepped forward to retrieve the basket, and as he picked it up, the inspector pulled his Webley and pointing it at the man's face, said, "You may eat your fill, but don't make a sound if you value your life."

Before the man could speak, Lestrade was on his feet, and Holmes and I were running to them. "Well done, Inspector," said Holmes.

Turning to Lestrade's captive, Holmes said, "I am going to ask you several questions. It will go much easier on you if you cooperate. Do you understand?"

The man nodded, so Holmes began. "Are you holding a prisoner on this ship?"

The guard nodded and replied, "Yes, sir."

"How many men are on board guarding him?"

"Just one other man, sir."

"Do you know the prisoner's name?"

"No sir," replied the man, growing more uneasy with each question.

"Why was the man kidnapped?"

"We were told he posed a threat to the King."

"What is the name of the other guard?"

"Dawkins, sir. Jimmy Dawkins."

"Last question," said Holmes. "Where is the prisoner being held?"

"He's two decks down, sir. Almost all the way up in the bow."

Turning to Lestrade, Holmes said, "Cuff him, Inspector. Watson and I shall be back shortly."

With that Holmes began walking up the gangplank and I followed him. Taking stock of the situation, I noticed for the first time that the ship was quite old. She was a full-rigged frigate that had obviously seen better days in the distant past. What remained of her sails were ripped and tattered, and the deck often creaked as we made our way towards the stern. The timbers were stained and worn, and there were more than a few gaping holes here and there where the wood had started to rot away.

Walking all the way to the rear of the ship, Holmes pulled open a hatch and began to descend a ladder. "Follow me, Watson, and be as silent as you can. Hopefully, we will enter the room where Mycroft is being held and the guard will be absent or asleep."

As we made our way forward, we found another ladder and descended into what must have once been the gun room but now looked more like a library. Next we entered a large pump room that appeared to have been transformed into a hospital ward. There were beds and bedpans scattered here and there as well as other medical detritus. Holmes bent down and removed his boots and indicated I should do the same. At the other end of the room was a set of doors, and it was easy to discern a light through the one door that was ajar.

Pressing his mouth to my ear, he whispered, "Now might be a good time to ready your sidearm." He then told me exactly what he wanted me to do. I followed his instructions to the letter and then watched in silence as Holmes crept up the side of the room until he was about five feet from the door, at which point, the boards creaked loudly under his feet.

The doors opened wide and a large man with a gun appeared. Training his weapon on Holmes, he said, "I don't know how you managed to get past Andy, but he's the last person you're ever going to get past. Who are you?"

"My name is Sherlock Holmes, and I believe you are Jimmy Dawkins. I also believe you are holding my brother prisoner."

"Well, Mr. Sherlock Holmes, I was told you might make an appearance. You had done better had you brought a pistol with you. And since you know my name and have seen my face, I'm afraid that makes things even worse for you."

"I see your point," replied my friend. "However, my friend is standing right behind you, and he did bring his gun. Does that square things?"

"You do yourself a disservice. If you think I'm going to fall for that old trick, I'd suggest you think again."

At that point, I stepped forward from my hiding place. Placing my revolver against the back of the man's skull, I said, "Lower your gun carefully and drop it on the deck."

Although I could not see it, Holmes later said the look of surprise on the thug's face was one he would never forget.

The man complied and Holmes pulled a length of rope from his pocket and soon had the man's wrists secured. I then went and summoned Lestrade, who joined us a few minutes later with his prisoner in tow.

We then entered the room and sitting on a chair in the corner was none other than Mycroft Holmes. His ankle had been chained to a bolt driven into the bulkhead. Although his head was covered with a black hood, there was no mistaking his considerable bulk.

From beneath the hood, Mycroft said, "Sherlock, is that you?"

Removing the black shroud, Holmes looked at his brother and said, "Surprisingly, you do not look much the worse for wear."

"It has been an interminable few days," said Mycroft. "I was rather hoping you would discover my message sooner rather than later."

"Unfortunately, that took somewhat longer than expected," replied Holmes. "I only just tumbled to it earlier today, and if truth be told, you owe your freedom to Dr. Watson."

At that, Mycroft turned to me and, after somehow managing a half-bow while still seated, said, "Thank you, Doctor. I shall never underestimate your abilities again. Nor shall I ever try to exclude you from any incident where I might need to call upon my brother for assistance."

Taking that small leather case from his pocket, Holmes extracted a tool, easily picked the lock, and then Mycroft was free.

"We must make our way to the reception," exclaimed Mycroft.

"And what will you do? What will you say?" asked Holmes. "Do you know who is responsible for your abduction?'

"I believe the spy in my office to be Geoffrey Langlois," exclaimed Mycroft.

"And why do you say that?" inquired Lestrade.

Glancing first at the inspector and then at his brother, Mycroft said, "He fell right into your trap. Of all my assistants, he was the only one to inquire about the Tenrev Brigade. On more than one occasion, he tried to insinuate the Brigade into our conversation, and I began to suspect him immediately."

"Well, your suspicions, as you might expect, were well-founded," said Holmes. "The only problem is Langlois is now dead, killed under rather suspicious circumstances in his own flat."

"My word," said Mycroft.

"I hope you appreciate the significance of his demise," said Holmes.

"Of course, I do," replied Mycroft rather quickly. "But I must admit that I am at something of a loss as to how to proceed – not having any recent data from which I might formulate a theory."

In the dim light, I thought I detected a wicked smile flash across my friend's face before he said, "Well, then isn't a good thing you have a younger brother." Holmes then began asking Mycroft a series of questions. When he had finished he looked at us all, smiled and said, "Now gentlemen, here is what's to be done."

Chapter 18

I cannot help but imagine there has always been a great degree of competition between the brothers Holmes. After my friend had finished outlining his plan, Mycroft began interrogating his younger brother about various points. Then they would both lapse into silence as they imagined other possible scenarios and outcomes.

Abruptly the quiet would be broken when one or the other would suddenly begin by saying, "Yes, but suppose ..." What followed then would be an elucidation of all the possibilities arrived at by that particular brother.

This process went on for well over an hour. Lestrade was doing his best to feign interest as was I, but those two were playing only to an audience of each other. After another thirty minutes of this verbal chess match, a few basics had been agreed upon, and I said, "Holmes, it is beginning to get late."

At that point, he looked at me and said, "Yes, quite right. Mycroft, we can continue this discussion tomorrow morning."

He then proceeded to issue instructions for all involved. "Lestrade, you will escort these two beauties to the Great Scotland Yard. Avoid the New Scotland Yard at all costs. Given your own predicament and everything that has transpired, we cannot vouch for the integrity of every officer on the force.

"Watson, you will escort Mycroft to the Diogenes Club. I want to you to enter via the rear door, Mycroft. Watson, make certain that nothing untoward happens during your journey."

"What are you going to be doing?" I asked.

"I will accompany Lestrade with his prisoners and then I have a few tasks to carry out. Although it is getting quite late, there is still no better time than the present to put my new plans into place."

I looked at Holmes, and I could see the excitement of the hunt on his flushed face. There was also a hint of relief. Although his quarry had proven resourceful and eluded him for quite some time, my friend appeared finally to have cornered his prey – or at the very least tracked it to its lair.

"Mycroft, we will meet you at the Diogenes at precisely 6 a.m.," he continued. "We shall have time for a quick breakfast as well as to review the decisions we have made this evening one last time. Lestrade, would you be so kind as to join us there?"

"It would be my great pleasure," said the Inspector.

With that we made our way off the ship and back towards Cloister Walk and the Tower Bridge. After several minutes of walking and two unsuccessful attempts at hailing a cab, Holmes was finally able to secure a dogcart near the bridge, and he quickly bundled Mycroft and me into it. I can only assume he wished to accompany Lestrade and the prisoners, lest the Inspector be outnumbered.

Mycroft and I made our way to the Diogenes Club, and per Holmes' instructions, we entered through the tradesmen's entrance in the rear. As you might expect, the valet who answered our knock was rather surprised to see Mycroft at the rear door, yet – per the rules of the club – he bowed and said not a word.

Before the door had closed, Mycroft, himself – ever-mindful of the prohibition against talking within the club – stepped back outside and once again expressed his gratitude to me, saying, "You have my deepest thanks, Dr. Watson. I shall see you, Lestrade, and my brother in the Stranger's Room at 6. Do not trouble yourself about breakfast; I shall have everything ready and waiting."

After warmly shaking my hand, he once again entered the club, and I jumped back into the cab and directed the driver to take me to Baker Street. It was obvious as I entered our darkened rooms that Holmes had yet to return. Well aware that we might have another long day in front of us, I decided to turn in. Although I feared I would not get much sleep – so concerned was I about oversleeping – that despite the best intentions, I tossed and turned much of the night before finally drifting off for a few hours.

As it turns out, I need not have concerned myself about oversleeping. I was roused from my slumber by a steady knocking at my door, and the voice of Holmes saying, "Watson? Watson?"

"Yes, Holmes. I am awake."

"*Tempus fugit*," was all he said.

I quickly dressed and performed my morning ablutions. The sun was just beginning to climb into the sky when I joined Holmes in our sitting room.

Despite the early hour, we managed to find a cab and directed the driver to take us to the Diogenes Club. Some short while later, we were sitting in the Stranger's Room with Lestrade and Mycroft enjoying a breakfast of bacon and eggs with kippers and some of the best coffee I have ever tasted.

Although Mycroft and Lestrade both attempted to elicit from Holmes what he expected from them, he remained close-mouthed until he had finished his breakfast.

Finally, after his third cup of coffee, he began to speak. "I have put in motion a plan to bring the spy to justice."

"You said Langlois was dead," replied Mycroft.

"And so he is," said Holmes. "So who killed him and why?"

"You don't mean …" said Mycroft, his words trailing off as he realized the full import of what his brother had said.

"I am afraid I do," replied my friend. "As Watson will attest, I never prepare just one plan of action. One must always allow for unexpected contingencies. Our former Prime Minister Benjamin Disraeli in his book *The Wondrous Tale of Alroy*, wrote, 'I am prepared for the worst, but hope for the best.' It is a motto I have adopted as my own, but apparently I am not the only one who believes in such thinking.

"Consider, how many years were spent in educating and grooming the man we knew as Geoffrey Langlois. Finally, Langlois is selected to assist the estimable Mycroft Holmes in making any number of governmental decisions.

"Suppose, however, that something unfortunate were to occur to Langlois – a robbery in his flat gone bad, a fatal carriage accident, a fall while riding – suddenly, that grand scheme would be for naught. So what's to be done?"

"A second spy?" inquired Lestrade.

"Exactly," replied Holmes.

"So I am twice duped!" exclaimed Mycroft.

"Do not be so hard on yourself, brother. I am certain their interests were advanced by any number of well-meaning officials – and perhaps a few with far more ignoble intentions."

"Do you know the identity of the second spy?" I asked.

"I have my suspicions, but at the moment I have no proof. However, I fully expect by this afternoon – this evening, at the latest – we shall have unmasked the traitor in our midst and restored things to their natural order."

"If you are successful, the British government will owe you a debt which it can never hope to repay, Sherlock," said Mycroft.

Ignoring his brother, Holmes asked, "Do you recall the agenda for the conference?"

"Indeed," said Mycroft. "Today was to be spent considering the most efficient manner in which each country might come to another's aid should it be attacked by a foreign power."

"I assume there were any number of documents and maps involved?"

"Yes," replied Mycroft. "Most were kept under lock and key in my safe and for those that had to be shared with my various assistants, we made copies."

"Excellent," exclaimed Holmes. "Now here is the plan of action which I have devised."

When he had finished explaining everything to us, there was absolute silence in the Stranger's Room. For those few minutes, we might have been sitting right in the center of any room in the Diogenes Club without attracting the least bit of attention."

Lestrade finally broke the stillness when he remarked, "I have said it before and I will say it again: Thank goodness, your inclinations never turned towards criminal endeavors, Mr. Holmes."

"If it works ..." said Mycroft who left the thought unfinished. After a few seconds, he said, "Do you have a backup plan for that contingency?"

Smiling ruefully, Holmes said, "Not at present, but I am trying to devise one as we speak."

At that, we all chuckled a bit although I must admit that Mycroft's laughter did strike me as rather forced.

Since it was now nearing 7:30, Holmes gave Lestrade and me our final instructions and then he and Mycroft departed for the latter's office.

As we stood on the sidewalk in the morning sun, watching them depart, Lestrade said to me, "I do hope this weather is an omen. Our friend has some rather strange ways, but, as I always say, the proof is in the pudding, and I would be hard-pressed to argue with his results."

"Indeed," I replied. "Holmes is always so concerned about someone giving something away prematurely that he would rather assume all the risk himself."

I looked at my watch and said, "It is just past the half hour. Since we have time to kill, shall we walk to the Arch?"

Lestrade agreed and the morning sun felt warm on my face as we strolled towards Hyde Park. We started on St. James Street and eventually turned on Half Moon Street which brought us to Curzon Street and then to Park Lane. Lestrade was obviously lost in his own thoughts as was I, so we continued in silence. At about quarter after eight, I saw the Arch in the distance.

Turning to Lestrade, I said, "You remember Holmes' instructions?"

"I certainly do," replied the inspector, "but I must confess that waiting has never been my strong suit."

When we arrived at the monument, I ascended to the top while Lestrade took up a post near the bronze gates under the center arch.

I climbed the stairs as quietly as I could and found Holmes and Mycroft there waiting for me. There are three small rooms inside the Arch. The largest of the three, presumably the barracks, had been cleared and three long tables had been arranged in the shape of a U.

"Things may become extremely close in here," remarked Mycroft. "I am wondering whether Doctor Watson might not be more comfortable waiting outside with Lestrade."

Turning to me, Holmes said, "I think Mycroft makes an excellent point." Turning back to his brother, he said, "And you know the proper time?"

"I should think so. Now go, before any of the others arrive and see you."

We walked through the rooms and descended the stairs. Exiting through the small door, we were soon joined by Lestrade.

"And now what happens?" asked the inspector.

"Now we maintain our vigil, gentlemen."

"For what, or perhaps should I say, for whom?" I asked.

Holmes gave me one of his rueful grins and said, "Certainly, you have come to the same conclusions as I."

Truth be told, I had not arrived at any conclusions at all, and I am afraid that my face must have given me away."

Gazing over my shoulder, Holmes said, "Here comes Mr. Cenk. Let us remove ourselves to a discreet distance and see how things play out. I will tell you there has been a change in plans. I had thought to bring this to a conclusion early this morning before the conference began, but Mycroft has offered a refinement to my scheme. Although I am not totally enamored of it, I can see where his suggestion suits his agenda far better than my simple denouement would have."

Lestrade looked at me and his face was the picture of exasperation. I nodded sympathetically and then shrugged my shoulders as if to say, "It is his decision."

And so we took seats on benches just inside the park from which we could keep an eye on the Arch. As you might expect, we all sat separately as Holmes thought three gentlemen sitting together on a park bench might arouse some degree of suspicion in even the most benighted passerby.

I will not bore the reader by detailing the arrival of the various delegations. Suffice to say they were small and inconspicuous as they surreptitiously slipped into the Arch and out of view.

After the Russian delegation, the last to arrive, had entered, Holmes stood and motioned Lestrade and me to him. "It is now a quarter past nine. Nothing will happen before noon. I have one more bit of business to which I must attend. Let us meet back here at a quarter to the hour, and then perhaps I can begin to sort things out for you gentlemen."

Lestrade harrumphed, and I could plainly see that he was annoyed; however, his demeanor quickly changed when Holmes said, "Inspector, by midday tomorrow, perhaps even sooner, barring anything unforeseen, you will once again be a member in good standing of the Metropolitan Police Force, and I shouldn't be at all surprised if you did not receive a commendation for your work on this case."

Although still in the dark, Lestrade smiled and said, "I never doubted you for a second Mr. Holmes. I shall meet you back here at the appointed time." With that the Inspector strode off, and I could swear I detected a slight jauntiness in his step as he exited the park.

"And what will you be doing for the next few hours?"

"I shall be returning *Cotton Vitellius A XV* to Dr. Smith. Would you care to join me?"

Chapter 19

Hailing a cab, Holmes directed the driver to take us to Baker Street. After we had settled into our seats, he explained, "I just have to collect something for Dr. Smith."

Holmes words stirred my memory, and I said, "In my bag, you will find the parcel which you asked me to deliver to Smith a week or so ago. If you wouldn't mind …"

My friend laughed, "I had quite forgotten about that. I would be happy to fetch it for you, Watson."

When we arrived at our lodgings, Holmes dashed upstairs, leaving the front door open, while I remained in the cab. In less than three minutes, he was once again seated opposite me. He handed me the smaller package. I say smaller because I noticed that under his arm he was carrying the large parcel which he had brought home with him to Baker Street several days ago.

Once we were underway, I broached the subject of how he had ascertained the location of the missing manuscript, but Holmes declined to answer my question. He would say only, "We have come this far. I think I deserve to ring down the curtain with a bit of a flourish, wouldn't you agree?"

Well aware of his penchant for the theatrical, I decided to humor my friend and possess my soul in patience until he had decided the time was right.

When we arrived at the museum, we were informed Dr. Smith was in, so we headed directly for his office.

Seated behind his desk, the historian rose when we entered. "I do hope that you bring good news, Mr. Holmes."

Looking at the academic, I could see that he appeared more haggard than I had ever seen him, and it was readily apparent that the missing manuscript had resulted in more than a few sleepless nights as well as a great deal of anxiety.

Holmes replied, "I am optimistic we will soon put this whole unpleasant business behind us. In the meantime, Watson and I have brought you something we hope may bring you some small degree of joy."

I must say I was quite touched that Holmes had included me, despite the fact that I had no idea what we had brought the good doctor.

Holmes motioned for me to hand the package to Smith.

"What is this?" he asked, his voice rising. "It's not the ...."

"No, Doctor Smith. It is not the *Nowell Codex*, but it is something that I hope will bring you many hours of pleasure as you peruse it. Now open it," said Holmes.

Smith tore open the paper and there was the copy of *Erewhon* by Samuel Butler that I had obtained for Holmes from Madame Cocilovo-Kozzi and her husband.

I could see Dr. Smith was touched by the gift.

"Mr. Holmes, I don't know how to thank you. I am quite fond of Butler, but I already have several copies of *Erewhon*."

"I am well aware of that," replied Holmes, "but I do not think you have a signed first edition."

Smith carefully opened the book and gazed at the title page with a mixture of fondness and astonishment. "How could you have known?"

Holmes laughed and said, "I should think the answer is fairly obvious."

"Not to me," I said.

"Nor me," added Smith.

Pointing to the bookcase behind Smith, Holmes said, "On that bottom shelf, all the way to the left is a copy of *The Way of All Flesh*; there on your desk is *The Authoress of the Odyssey,* which has taken the place of Butler's *Shakespeare's Sonnets Reconsidered.* Three books by the same author might suggest a certain fondness, but on past visits here I have seen other titles by Mr. Butler, both on your desk and on your shelves."

"My word, Mr. Holmes."

"Wait until he starts to read your mind then you will be really amazed," I offered.

Holmes then brought us back to the present, "Now, if we may, I should like to pay one more visit to the rare book room."

As we were approaching the King's Library a few minutes later, I saw the guard sitting at his desk. He looked up as we approached, "Ah, Dr. Smith, what brings you down here? And Mr. Holmes, it is a pleasure to see you again."

Holmes said, "You are looking well, Mr. Green. Allow me to present my friend and colleague, Dr. John Watson."

After we had exchanged pleasantries, Green unlocked the door for us, giving Holmes a rather wry look.

"Is there something amiss, Mr. Green?" asked Holmes.

"Normally, I inspect all packages going into the room, but as you're with Dr. Smith, I don't suppose that will be necessary."

"Quite right," said Dr. Smith.

"Nonsense," interjected Holmes. "Please do your duty, and treat me as you would any other visitor." And with that he handed his parcel to Green, who placed it on his desk and carefully unwrapped it, revealing an oversized Volume I of Dr. Johnson's Dictionary.

"Blimey!" exclaimed Green, "Another copy of Dr. Johnson's Dictionary! This book just can't seem to stay out of this room."

I then remembered the academic who had visited the room for several days shortly before the *Nowell Codex* disappeared. I also recalled Holmes dispatching me to obtain the book's measurements. I watched as Green examined the book, flipping some of the pages, before returning it to Holmes.

"I'm sorry to have troubled you Mr. Holmes."

"No trouble at all," replied my friend. We then entered the room, and Holmes promptly placed the book on the nearest reading table.

"Now, Dr. Smith, I am going to tell you exactly what I think happened to the *Beowulf* manuscript." Moving to the case where the manuscript had been kept, Holmes reached into his jacket pocket. "I seem to have forgot my lens. Is there one here, Dr. Smith?"

"Let me check." Smith then rummaged through the drawers of several desks before turning to us with an apologetic look. "There are usually two or three here, but not to worry, I have one in my desk. Just let me fetch it."

After Smith had departed, I looked at Holmes and said, "What are you up to, old man?"

"Just a bit of the theatrical that you accuse me of being so fond of. Now, do hand me your pen knife?"

I reached into my pocket, and it wasn't there. "In the early morning rush, I must have left it at home."

"See if Mr. Green has one, would you?"

I went out to the guard and relayed Holmes' request. "I have one here somewhere," he replied as he sifted through the detritus that had collected in his various desk drawers. While he was searching, I heard footsteps in the hall and turned to see Dr. Smith returning with the lens. "Would you happen to have a pen knife as well? Holmes is looking for one."

"Certainly," he replied, pulling a sterling silver blade from his pocket. "This was a gift from my father, and I am never without it."

We re-entered the rare book room and found Holmes lounging languidly in one of the reading chairs.

As we entered, he stood up and took the lens and knife from Smith. "You may recall that on our first visit here after the book was discovered missing, I examined the case, paying particular attention to the lock. Dr. Smith, I encourage you to take another look at the lock."

After handing Smith his lens, Holmes stepped aside. Smith then stepped to the case and the only word that can describe the sound the man made next is a shriek. Turning my attention to the case, I saw a weathered, leather-bound volume reposing on the brilliant green velvet that lined the bottom of the display."

After tasking a moment to compose himself, Smith finally began to utter an intelligible sentence.

"But how, Mr. Holmes? Where did this come from? You are truly a magician."

At the last word, I saw a brief smile on Holmes face and rather than say anything, I allowed him his moment of adulation.

"Let me begin at the beginning," said Holmes. "When we first discussed the missing *Codex*, you made a point of telling me how dependable Mr. Green is. In point of fact, you saw for yourself just a few minutes ago how diligent he is. That set me to thinking that anyone attempting to spirit the book out of here would run a terrible risk.

"So they set about employing a stratagem in order to create the illusion that the book had been taken."

"How could they do that?" Smith asked.

Pointing to the copy he had brought, Holmes said, "Watson, if you would be so kind as to hand me that copy of Dr. Johnson's Dictionary."

I went to the table and picked it up, only to discover that it was far lighter than I had expected. "Holmes, this book doesn't weigh nearly as much as it should."

"And there we have it," my friend replied.

Taking the book, he thumbed through a number of pages and then he turned to show us the last page. As he flipped it over, I saw that the last three-quarters of the several hundred pages had been hollowed out.

"During my investigation into rare book dealers, I discovered that a man – the same man, in fact – had purchased two copies of Volume I of Dr. Johnson's Dictionary – without purchasing a second volume – which was also readily available in both instances. That set me to thinking. Why would someone require two copies of the same book? And for quite a pretty penny, I might add. Obviously, one had to be disposable. On an unannounced visit here, I examined the copy of the dictionary that was residing on the shelf and discovered the *Nowell Codex* had been carefully concealed inside the first volume."

Turning to Smith, Holmes said, "Dr. Smith, I owe you an apology. I could have eased your mind two weeks ago, but there are other, far more important, forces at play here. I needed you to keep believing the *Beowulf* manuscript was missing because I did not know if they were watching you. Any change in your demeanor might have communicated to them the book was safe."

"Mr. Holmes, if you say you had a good reason, I trust you. That you have recovered it is the important thing."

"But why two dictionaries, Holmes?" I asked.

"During the first several visits by the bogus professor, he brought the uncut dictionary. If Mr. Green had examined it, as I am certain he did, he would discover nothing unusual. Eventually, I suspect, the dull routine of daily existence caught up with Mr. Green. Looking at the same book day after day, he saw what he had already seen several times – more importantly, he saw what he expected to see.

"On the professor's final visit, he took a chance. I am certain Mr. Green gave the volume a cursory examination, as he had done every day that week. However, on that day, the professor entered carrying the hollowed out dictionary. He placed the *Codex* inside it and placed it back on the shelf, he then left carrying your copy of the dictionary – complete and whole."

"But why, Mr. Holmes?"

"To keep me busy. To distract me from something far more crucial." Looking at his watch, Holmes said, "And that something is calling to me now. Dr. Smith, we must be on our way. However, I would suggest that you purchase a new display case for the *Codex* and have it fitted with shatterproof glass and the latest Chubb lock. I hear they are *almost* impossible to pick."

With that, we left Dr. Smith in the rare book room, bid farewell to Silas Green and made our way out of the museum.

When we were safely ensconced in the cab and heading for the Marble Arch, I said to Holmes, "I assume Mr. Green was a partner in today's production?"

Rather than answer, Holmes merely smiled enigmatically and said, "As were you?"

"Me?"

Grinning, Holmes reached into his pocket, pulled out a small object and said, "I believe this belongs to you." With that he returned my own pen knife to me. "I took the liberty of 'borrowing' it from your pocket earlier this morning."

"Holmes, you rascal."

Everything had fallen into place but one thing. After a few minutes, I said, "I understand why you did everything you did, but I still think keeping Dr. Smith in the dark still seems rather cruel in retrospect."

My friend smiled and said softly, "Like you, Dr. Smith cannot mask his emotions. I assure you it gave me no pleasure to keep the location of the book from him, but had he known – and acted differently – things might have taken a very nasty turn.

"I can only hope that the rest of this case resolves itself as smoothly as that aspect did."

"You sound as though you are still concerned."

"Consider, Watson. These men have threatened my life, killed Langlois and kidnapped Mycroft. I shall remain 'concerned' – and vigilant – until justice has been served."

Chapter 20

Holmes then placed his chin on his chest and said nothing more, as was his wont at such times. As a result, we spent the rest of the ride in silence. When we stepped down from the cab at the entrance to Hyde Park, I saw Lestrade had returned to his previous post. Glancing at my watch, I was surprised to see that it was close upon the quarter hour.

We met Lestrade about halfway between his earlier position and the Arch. Looking at Holmes, the Inspector said, "It is almost quarter to. I have been here for at least ten minutes, and no one has entered or left the conference."

"Nor will they until noon at the earliest," replied my friend. "That is the hour my brother has designated for lunch. He had originally thought to have food and drink brought in so they might continue the work uninterrupted. However, I convinced him that, at least for today, if the plan were to work, an opportunity must be provided."

Before I could ask, "An opportunity for what?" we were joined by Wiggins.

"Gentlemen," said Wiggins, tipping his cap to the three of us. "Everything 'as been arranged just the way you wanted it, Mr. 'Olmes."

"Well done, Wiggins. This is for the lads," said my friend as he extracted several notes from his wallet. "I shall be awaiting your report."

"As soon as we 'ave it, you shall 'ave it, Mr. 'Olmes," replied Wiggins who then sauntered off back towards Park Lane.

Pulling out his pocket watch, Holmes said, "It is now ten of the hour; let us retire to our benches and see what transpires, shall we?"

Fortunately, the benches which Holmes and I had sat on earlier were still unoccupied. Facing a choice between sharing a bench with a nanny watching over an infant in a pram, Lestrade chose, as I would have, a seat a bit further from the Arch.

With nothing to occupy me, except my thoughts, those next ten minutes seemed an eternity. Finally, I saw the door open and three men, whom I knew to be the French delegation, step out into the noonday sun. As they stood there, allowing their eyes to adjust to the brilliant daylight, they were joined by the four-member

Russian delegation. And a minute later, Mycroft and his trio of assistants emerged.

They walked to the curb where four growlers were waiting to take them to lunch. After they had all boarded, the growlers began their journey down Oxford Street when the final one stopped at the end of the block. Young Dennison jumped down, and while I could see him saying something, first to the passengers and then the driver, I was too far away make out any of the words. After he had spoken, the carriages continued on their way.

Dennison returned to the Arch and entered it, and then a short while later he reappeared, carrying a briefcase that he had not had moments earlier. Holmes nodded discreetly at Lestrade. I watched in amazement as Dennison crossed Park Lane and started down that thoroughfare in the general direction of the Thames, seemingly totally unaware that he was being tailed by Lestrade, walking some fifty years behind him.

Were it not for the fact that Dennison was heading in a totally different direction from the route taken by the growlers, it might have seemed a thoroughly unremarkable event. A young man retrieving his briefcase and then heading somewhere nearby for lunch; however, I knew there was far more to it than that.

I walked over to Holmes and said, "I see you have Lestrade keeping tabs on young Dennison. Aren't you going to do anything?"

"Indeed, I am. First, I am going to finish this cigarette, then I am going to return to our rooms and await word of any developments."

"And you aren't going to tell me anything, are you?"

Drawing on his cigarette, he smiled and said, "All in good time, Watson. I would hate to bore you by subjecting you to the same story twice or perhaps even thrice."

"I could always leave the room, you know."

Ignoring my remark, Holmes finished his cigarette and then said, "I am feeling rather hungry; I do hope Mrs. Hudson has prepared something savory for lunch."

Knowing to press him would be futile, I fell in beside him. Truly, the man could try anyone's patience.

Later that evening, we had settled into our chairs when I heard the bell, and a few minutes later, I discerned footfalls on the steps.

"Pour Lestrade a brandy, will you, Watson?"

I didn't bother to ask, and a minute later, there was a knock on the door.

"Come in, Lestrade. We have been awaiting your arrival with bated breath. At least, Watson has."

I handed Lestrade his drink, and he took the chair in which Holmes' clients often sat. After he had settled himself, Holmes said, "And how did you fare with young Dennison?"

"Oh, he led us a merry chase, he did, but between my efforts and those of your Irregulars, we managed not to lose sight of him. By the way, that Wiggins is a very sharp customer. I don't suppose he has any interest in joining the Yard."

At that Holmes laughed heartily, "I am inclined to doubt it, but I shall tell him to drop round and see you, and you may ask him yourself."

"At any rate," continued Lestrade, "I followed Dennison down Park Lane where he eventually hailed a cab. I followed that across the river to a pub, The Three Roosters, in Croydon. After entering, he had a long conversation with the barman, who I later learned is the owner. Dennison then went upstairs. I can only assume he has maintained a room there.

"Perhaps twenty minutes later, he came out of the pub dressed as a rather disreputable laborer. He made two more stops at a florist and a greengrocer – the addresses of which I have copied here in my notebook."

"Well done, Lestrade. And you are certain you were not observed?"

"The only ones who saw me were your lads, and they seemed to be everywhere," said Lestrade.

"Given what I suspected, I rather anticipated this move by Dennison; as a result, I was able to station Irregulars in all the areas to which I suspected Dennison might bolt. Given Wiggins' reports, Croydon was at the top of my list."

I was just about to ask Holmes how he ascertained that Dennison was the second spy when the bell sounded again.

"Ah, that would be Mycroft's man," remarked Holmes. Looking at me, he said, "I know that you must have a million questions, and I promise you that all will be revealed in very short order. Now, gentlemen, I believe my brother is awaiting our arrival."

We descended the stairs to find a handsome Clarence waiting for us with a driver in grey livery. Drawn by two all black stallions, the carriage was quite obviously owned by the government. The interior was every bit as plush as the exterior, and I must admit to being a bit remorseful when the brief ride was over.

After entering the club, we were once again escorted to the Stranger's Room, where, a few moments later, we were joined by Mycroft. Looking none the worse for wear as a result of his recent ordeal, he seemed almost jovial – if such a term could ever be applied to Mycroft Holmes.

"Good evening," he said as he entered. Gazing about, he remarked, "I see that we are still one short."

"Who is missing?" I asked.

"In due time, Doctor Watson," replied Mycroft.

"I should think the answer were obvious," said Holmes.

I remember thinking to myself, although physically different, they are more alike than they realize.

At that moment, Sir Henry Campbell-Bannerman entered the Stranger's Room. "I do apologize for my tardiness, but there was a slight matter in Whitehall that demanded my attention."

"More unrest in Belfast?" inquired Mycroft.

The Prime Minister gazed at him with a certain degree of awe. "Exactly," he said. "We shall take it up tomorrow."

He continued, "Now, I should like to hear exactly what transpired at your conference today." Looking at Holmes, Lestrade and myself, he said, "I know that I can trust you gentlemen, but just a reminder that anything you hear is not for public consumption."

"They are models of discretion, I assure you," said Mycroft, and then turning to his younger brother, he said, "The stage is yours, Sherlock."

Chapter 21

"As I often instruct my clients to do, I shall begin at the beginning," said Holmes, as he filled his pipe.

He then recounted his adventure in Paris and his suspicion that there might be a spy in the government. "Having arrived at that conclusion, I suddenly found myself besieged by cases – two of which involved old friends – and all of which seemed to demand my personal and immediate attention. In fact, they even dispatched a woman in an attempt to lure us from London by appealing to Dr. Watson's well-documented sense of chivalry."

My comment about the woman in question being "quite a fetching lass" drew a laugh from the others and a quick glance of disapproval from Holmes, who, otherwise ignored my remark and continued, "As you probably know, I cannot abide boredom, and now I was suddenly beset by a number of tasks which Watson, in one of his more poetic flourishes, compared to the Labors of Hercules."

He then related our efforts on behalf of Lestrade and how the desk and safe in the warehouse had allegedly been purchased by Mycroft and the good inspector himself, respectively. "I think the fact that this group had the audacity to tweak me spurred me on to even greater efforts," he added.

"I knew we were finally making real progress when Mycroft was abducted. The question was in which direction to proceed. When Wiggins first informed me of Langlois' daily visits to the park – sometimes with a newspaper and sometimes without – I devised a scheme to confront our adversary in the Whispering Gallery.

"I suspected Langlois had an cohort, and when Langlois turned up dead and the meeting at St. Paul's proved an utter fiasco, I suddenly realized he had at least two associates. In fact, at that point, I began to think he was merely part of a much larger ring. The question remained how to ferret them out.

"After I discovered the existence of a second warehouse – one of which had allegedly been leased by Dennison and the other by Deniz Cenk – I determined that a visit to the second warehouse was in order.

Holmes then described his search and how he tumbled to the clue left by Mycroft. "That was very clever of you, Mycroft."

"It was fortunate they didn't take my watch nor the key on my fob. I made the scratches in the wood using the key. While I was feigning sleep, I overheard them say where they were planning to take me next."

At that point I interrupted, "But you said the marks spelled out HM 5 MEN. How did you make the jump to a ship – especially when you thought Mycroft had inverted his initials?"

"Did you really think that, Sherlock?" Mycroft asked, disapproval in his voice.

"Just for a very brief while," Holmes admitted. "However it might have been much longer were it not for Dr. Watson."

"Me?" I inquired.

"Do you remember your remark in the cab?" asked Holmes.

"Something about a long journey with twists and turns." I replied.

"'Sing to me of the man, Muse, the man of twists and turns,' is the first line of 'The Odyssey.' At that point, I realized that Mycroft had not inverted his initials and that the 5 was actually intended to be an S. After leaving you, Watson, I paid a visit to the harbormaster who informed me that there was a ship, the HMS Menelaus, once a battle frigate and a later a hospital ship and then a prison hulk, now rotting at the wharf by St. Katharine's Dock.

"You all know the story from that point on," said Holmes.

"But why did you miss the meeting after assuring me that you would be there?" asked Sir Henry.

"There were two reasons. First, I wanted to convey the impression that I was fully complying with their demands by absenting myself from the meeting. Second, believing the spy would be tied up indefinitely allowed me to pursue several avenues of my own. Unfortunately, none of them panned out. As a result, I was forced to reconsider everything which had transpired, albeit from a slightly different perspective. There is something to be said for a long night of reflection and several pipes of shag."

"And what was all the rigmarole about maps in the Diogenes Club?" asked Lestrade.

"Mycroft, would you care to explain?" Holmes said.

Taking up the story, Mycroft began, "By that time, we knew that the second spy was another of my assistants. I was inclined to think it might be Cenk, but Sherlock, I knew, had cast his net elsewhere.

"At any rate, we retired to my office that morning where I constructed an entirely fictitious set of maps and diagrams showing our present and planned fortifications as well as our existing and potential supply lines, with notes in the margin, indicating the number of days it would take us to respond to any sort of outbreak of hostilities on the continent. As you have probably surmised, they were for the most part false."

"Yes, yes, I see that," said the Prime Minister, "but how could you possibly know that the spy would respond as he did?"

"My sudden appearance at the meeting was, I am sure, a trifle unnerving for young Mister Dennison. Still, I will give the man credit; he never flinched when I entered the room."

"Yes, but how did you know that he would take the bait and bolt?"

"Sherlock?" said Mycroft.

Smiling broadly, my friend continued the narrative, "After we had left the Menelaus and I had deposited Lestrade and his prisoners at Scotland Yard, I picked up three copies of The Times, one for each assistant, and then inserted a coded message in each. Of course, it would only make sense to one."

"What did the message say?" asked Lestrade.

"'Fear detection. Take what you can. Leave at noon'," replied Holmes.

"So that explains Dennison's sudden return to the Arch," I said.

"Yes," Holmes continued, "thinking he was about to be discovered, he took advantage of the break for lunch to return, collect all of Mycroft's papers and flee."

"But not before making a few stops," added Lestrade. "We now have the names of several of his contacts, and you can bet we will be keeping a close eye on them in the future."

At that point, Sir Henry looked right at Holmes and said, "You let him escape on purpose?"

Mycroft answered, "That was a joint decision reached by Sherlock and myself. We thought it better to let him go free with the false plans – learning the identities of his contacts was an added bonus – than to have him rot in an English gaol and tell us nothing. There is no way to estimate what type of havoc those maps and diagrams will wreak, but I am inclined to hope it will be substantial."

"But how did you tumble to Dennison?" I asked.

"Mycroft initially thought the spy to be Langlois," said Holmes, "and he was correct in that respect. The proof was in the fact that Langlois was the assistant who kept bringing up the Tenrev Brigade. I rather suspect Dennison was the driving force behind his inquiries."

"Yes, but how did you arrive at Dennison?" I persisted.

"I eliminated Cenk after observing him with his wife and children. Not even the best spy could feign the obvious affection he demonstrated when with them. That left Dennison and Bern. The scales began to shift in Dennison's favor after he visited us at Baker Street."

"Yes, but one of the warehouses had been leased in his name. Why would he do that?"

"A very clever ploy. If you recall, he involved himself and Cenk, but not Langlois and Bern. I am certain somewhere out there, waiting to be discovered, is a document of some sort linking Langlois to this affair. If Dennison were questioned or suspected, I believe he would have somehow led us to those documents, thus lumping himself in with the innocent Cenk and the not-so-innocent Langlois, leaving Bern all by himself to take the fall."

"One last question," said Lestrade, "Why kill Langlois?"

"As to the motive behind that, I can but speculate. Perhaps he was beginning to lose his nerve although I am far more inclined to think they believed such a sacrifice might occupy me to the point where I would shift my attention to the murder and perhaps allow them to complete their rather nefarious plans."

"Well, do you have any idea who killed him?"

"Were I forced to guess, I should put my money on one Otto Kueck, a member of the *Ettappendienst der Marine*, a sort of German secret service, as the mastermind behind this whole plot. He returned to Germany last year after spending several years as vice counsel in the Mexican state of Chihuahua. I had heard that he was suffering from some sort of liver illness, but I have to believe he has recovered by now.

"You will recall Watson, I drew your attention to the different types of tobacco in the ashtray in Langlois' apartment. I easily discerned the types of tobacco ash that had been left by his cigarettes and cigars. I could find nothing in his room to explain the third, so it was obvious Langlois had entertained a visitor who was also a smoker. As for the keys in Langlois pocket, his house

298

key was right there along with the others. I checked all the keys on the door while you and Lestrade were searching the rest of the building. You will recall when we knocked on the door, it was locked. Someone, whom Langlois obviously trusted, had a set of keys to his flat which they locked after killing him. I can only assume it was Dennison, and at some point, he passed them to Kueck."

"And the reading glasses?" I asked.

"On our first visit to Mycroft's office, Langlois took his seat after introducing himself and immediately resumed reading the papers before him sans spectacles. On none of his visits to the park, was he observed wearing glasses while reading the paper.

"I am inclined to think the case was somehow used to conceal and carry messages. I should not be surprised, were we to capture Kueck, if we did not discover an identical case among his possessions."

"My word, Holmes. That certainly does appear to cover everything."

"Well, I will inform my friends at the Yard and they will certainly set their caps for this Kueck fellow," said Lestrade.

"I should think he too has left England, but you may do your best," remarked Holmes.

Breaking into the conversation, Sir Henry said, "Thank you for reminding me, Mr. Holmes. Inspector. I have something for you." Pulling an envelope from his inside jacket pocket, he handed it to Lestrade. "That is a letter signed by myself and Commissioner Edward Henry clearing you of all charges and ordering the lifting of your suspension and your reinstatement, effective immediately."

After expressing his gratitude to the Prime Minister, Lestrade turned to Holmes and said, "You've never let me down, Mr. Holmes. Thank you."

Holmes continued answering questions for another ten minutes before the interrogation ceased. Looking about, he said, "Well, gentlemen, I believe that concludes our business this evening, I know that both Lestrade and Mycroft have an early day tomorrow, and there is the little matter of a set designer's sudden disappearance in the West End that clamors for my attention."

After exchanging pleasantries, Holmes and I were soon in a cab bound for Baker Street. When we had reached the sitting room, Holmes looked at me and said, "Would you care for a nightcap?"

As we sat in our chairs, sipping brandy and smoking the last pipe of the day, I turned to Holmes and said, "I do have one more question."

"Just one?" he teased.

"Do you know whatever became of the woman who visited here?"

"I assume you are referring to the lady who presented herself as Deborah Werth from Shropshire."

"Yes, I am."

"She is currently appearing as Rosalind in a revival of the Bard's *As You Like It* at the Hackney Theatre."

"How the deuce did you discover that?"

"While your head is easily turned by a trim waist and a beguiling smile, I am not so easily swayed. Since she had no idea I would be absent when she called here, I was inclined to think she might be a professional actress. I had the Irregulars scour the theatres until they encountered a young woman fitting her description. I then paid a call upon her one evening before her performance. However, I must admit that I am rather disappointed in you in this one instance, Watson. I left the name of the theatre on the table for you to find."

"But I had no idea what it meant," I said in my own defense.

"Nor did you attempt to elicit the meaning," he laughed. "At any rate, that is all water under the bridge. When I visited the young lady and told her who I was, she immediately asked, 'So who won the bet?' She believed that she had been hired by my brother to present us with a case that we could not possibly solve – since, in fact, there really was no case to speak of. I refrained from disabusing her of the notion and simply said, 'My brother.' I must admit Watson, she is charming and as you stated earlier this evening 'quite fetching.'" He paused before adding, "I do believe those to be your exact words."

"Dash it all, Holmes. Do you ever forget anything?"

He smiled and reaching into his jacket pocket extracted an envelope. "I have two front row seats for tomorrow night's performance of *As You Like It*, should you care to attend."

Laughing, I said, "Nothing would delight me more."

Epilogue

I cannot say with any degree of certainty whether Mycroft's secret conference was able to delay the outbreak of hostilities. Nor can I offer an opinion as to whether the bogus maps and diagrams with which young Dennison escaped were able to play any role in the fighting once hostilities had commenced. I like to comfort myself by thinking that our plans resulted in at least a few lives having been saved.

At any rate, war did not break out until seven years later. Looking back, who would have thought that the bullets fired by a teenager which struck and killed an Austrian nobleman, who had engaged in a morganatic marriage, would be the match that let the fuse?

Who could have imagined that less than a month after Archduke Franz Ferdinand's assassination, the continent would be embroiled in "the war to end all wars?" Who could have foreseen that Britain's attempts to mediate the conflict would be rebuffed and that we would enter the war that August to defend Belgium?

Had you told anyone in 1907 that less than a decade later millions upon millions of people – mostly young men in their prime – would die and that millions upon millions more – from all walks of life and of all ages – would be wounded, that person would have scoffed at such a notion. After all, we were civilized, enlightened. We had entered the twentieth century.

Thoughts of poison gas, flamethrowers and aerial combat – all of which were developed during the course of that conflict – were rarities in 1907 as was the notion of trench warfare. My heart aches when I think of the lives lost in "No Man's Land" and the unchecked barbarity that man exhibited towards his brothers.

We struggled to avoid war and despite our best efforts, it occurred, and the toll – in terms of suffering, misery and loss of life – can never really be reckoned. It is beyond sobering to think of an entire generation lost, and, in the final analysis, for what?

My ardent hope, as we prepare for a new year, is that we finally learn from this terrible lesson and take steps to make certain such a cataclysm never occurs again.

Your humble and obedient servant,

Dr. John H. Watson

31 December 1918

Author's notes

In college and then in graduate school, I have always been fascinated by medieval English literature. The story of the survival of *Cotton Vitellius A XV* is an astounding one, and I have tried to convey just how fortunate we are that the manuscript withstood all the myriad forces that seemed bent on its destruction. (On this point, however, I willingly admit some of my former students might disagree heartily.)

The Whispering Gallery at St. Paul's Cathedral is one of those architectural oddities that definitely deserves a visit should you ever find yourself in London. For those for whom all knowledge is grist for their mill, I can recommend Lord Rayleigh's "The Theory of Sound." Although I cannot even pretend to understand most of it, the section on the Whispering Gallery is fascinating.

The *HMS Menelaus* was a Royal Navy 38-gun fifth-rate frigate that entered service in 1810 at Plymouth. She saw action in the war of 1812, raiding American positions along the eastern coastline. She also took part in the Battle of Baltimore. In 1820 she moved to Chatham and in 1832 was transformed into a hospital ship, becoming the quarantine ship at Sandgate Street. In December 1848, she accepted sick inmates from the convict ship *Hasemey*, which qualified her to be listed among the infamous prison "Hulks." She remained with the Quarantine Service until 1890. In 1897, she was sold for the last time.

With regard to the title of Prime Minister, there would seem to be no specific date for when the office of prime minister first appeared. History tells us that the position was not created but rather evolved over a period of time through a merger of different duties. Still, the term was regularly, if informally, used of Sir Robert Walpole by the 1730s. It was also used in the House of Commons at the beginning of the 19th century and appears to have gained currency in Parliamentary use by the 1880s. However, it was not until 1905 that the post of prime minister was officially given recognition in the order of precedence. Although most modern historians generally regard Walpole, who led the government for more than two decades, and thus is also longest serving prime minister, it can be argued that Sir Henry Campbell-Bannerman was the first prime minister officially referred to as such in the order of precedence.

Chubb locks are mentioned in both "A Scandal in Bohemia" and "The Golden Pince-Nez." They continued to be manufactured under that name until 2010 when the license was not renewed. The locks are still produced under the names Yale and Union, and as the new manufacturer likes to say, the locks are still "Chubb at Heart."

At one time the Lebus Furniture Company could lay claim to being the largest furniture factory in the world. The firm started out producing desks and other pieces, but in World War I, the firm produced, among other things, wooden ammunition boxes. In World War II, the furniture was shunted aside as the company was called upon to produce a number of different types of aircraft for the government. The firm eventually closed its doors in 1969.

Acknowledgements

Of the five Sherlock Holmes novels I have now written, I must admit this was far and away the most taxing.

Since my stories take me where they want to go, I often find myself painted into a corner, and I am forced to put the writing process on hold until I can devise some way to escape my predicament. In this novel, it seems as though there were many more corners from which I had to extricate myself than in my previous efforts.

Fortunately, I have a wonderful support network whose members have learned that there is usually a method behind my seemingly "mad" questions, and who tolerate and even courage me despite the late hours at which such questions are often posed.

Topping the list is my wife, Grace, who continues to believe in me even as I continue to be filled with doubts about my own ability. Without her unflagging encouragement, I would probably never have become a writer, and because of her I persevere in this lonely task.

I also owe a big debt to my older brother, Edward. Having spent much of his adult life living in England and Scotland, he has often proven to be an invaluable resource. In that same vein, Deborah Annakin Peters, who was born and raised in Great Britain, has saved me from any number of linguistic and stylistic gaffes.

I should be terribly remiss if I failed to thank my publisher, Steve Emecz, who continues to make the process as painless as possible, and Brian Belanger, whose skill as a cover designer remains unmatched.

Also providing invaluable assistance was Lynn Johnson, the head of the Visitor Experience Center at St. Paul's Cathedral in London. She filled in some gaping holes about the famed Whispering Gallery for me.

A very special thanks to Jason Jones of Key Elements Safe Engineers in Essex, who provided a great deal of invaluable information about Chubb safes and locks.

I also owe a considerable debt to Bob Katz, a good friend and mentor, who remains the finest Sherlockian I know. He has continued to encourage me and is kind enough to read my efforts with an eye towards accuracy – both with regard to the Canon, and perhaps more importantly, to common sense.

As always a special thanks to Francine and Richard Kitts, both fine Sherlockians, for their unflagging support and encouragement.

A very special thanks to the Hesburgh Library at the University of Notre Dame. As a graduate student, I was allowed to borrow an early two-volume edition of Dr. Johnson's Dictionary. Those massive tomes remained in my dorm room for several weeks while I labored on a term paper, and after I returned them and pointed out their significance, they soon found a new home among that library's special collections.

Finally, to all those, and there are far too many to name, whose support for my earlier efforts has provided a spark of encouragement in my darkest moments of self-doubt, a heartfelt thank you.

About the author

Richard T. Ryan is a native New Yorker, having been born and raised on Staten Island. He majored in English at St. Peter's College in Jersey City and pursued his graduate studies, concentrating on medieval literature, at the University of Notre Dame in Indiana.

After teaching high school and college for several years, he joined the staff of the Staten Island Advance newspaper. He worked there for nearly 30 years, rising through the ranks to become news editor. When he retired in 2016, he held the title of publications manager for that paper although he still prefers the title, news editor.

In addition to his first novel, "The Vatican Cameos: A Sherlock Holmes Adventure," he has written several other Holmes' pastiches, including "The Stone of Destiny," "The Druid of Death" and "The Merchant of Menace." He has also penned three trivia books, including "The Official Sherlock Holmes Trivia Book."

In a different medium, he can also boast of having "Deadly Relations," a mystery-thriller, produced off-Broadway on two separate occasions.

And if that weren't enough, he is also the very proud father of two children, Dr. Kaitlin Ryan-Smith and Michael Ryan, and the incredibly proud grandfather of Riley Grace.

He has been married for more than 40 years to his long-suffering wife, Grace, who, fortunately is far more computer literate and has far more patience than he. They live together with Homer, a black Lab mix, who is the real king of the Ryan castle.

He is currently at work on his next Holmes' pastiche as well as a period piece set in the Middle Ages – a temporary departure from the Great Detective. After that, he plans to delve once again into the box he purchased at auction and see what tales remain.

For a preview of his latest Holmes work, see below.

Three May Keep a Secret
A Sherlock Holmes Adventure

By Richard T. Ryan

Chapter 1

Of the many adventures that I shared with my friend, Sherlock Holmes during our years together, I am not certain that any had a stranger beginning than that which involved the late Ralph Prescott.

The events that make up the bulk of the case began in the summer of 1894, shortly after Holmes' miraculous resurrection from the waters at the bottom of the Reichenbach Falls. As you might expect, upon his return from the "dead" and following the apprehension of Colonel Sebastian Moran, he had been besieged with cases and displaying his usual preference for the *outre,* he had refused to accept the vast majority of them, describing most of them as "mundane" or proclaiming for others that the solution was "patently self-evident."

One morning in late July, I stopped by to visit my friend. As you might expect, my practice slowed considerably during the summer months, and as my wife had a social engagement that afternoon, I made my way from Queen Anne Street to my old haunt at 221B after seeing the last of my patients in the morning.

Holmes looked well, and we were chatting amicably as he informed me of his latest exploits when our long-suffering landlady knocked on our door. In his usual brusque manner, Holmes replied, "Come in, Mrs. Hudson."

She entered clutching a small envelope and said, "I am so sorry to disturb you gentlemen, but this just arrived by messenger for you, Mr. Holmes."

Taking it from her, he opened it, and as she turned to leave, he said, "Mrs. Hudson, if you please."

After perusing it twice, Holmes looked at her and said, "Kindly inform the messenger I will not be at home at the appointed hour, and please stress I am not accepting any new cases at the moment."

"I would, sir," she replied, "but the messenger didn't wait for a reply. He simply delivered the envelope, and then he hopped on his bicycle and pedaled off towards Marylebone Road."

"Thank you, Mrs. Hudson. That will be all."

"What does it say, Holmes?"

He then handed me a single sheet of note paper, which had been folded in half. Upon opening it, I read the following.

Dear Mr. Holmes,

I shall call upon you this afternoon precisely at four o'clock. I expect you will make yourself available as it is a matter of some urgency – and delicacy.

I look forward to making your acquaintance.

Sincerely,

Ralph Prescott

"What do you make of it, Holmes?"

"Actually, I make rather little of it. The paper is of exceptionally fine quality and quite costly. The writer has employed a high-quality fountain pen, perhaps a Waterman or a Wirk, although I am inclined to lean towards the former. The hand which composed the note is strong and confident. Further, Mr. Prescott has gone through the additional expense of having had it delivered by messenger rather than post.

"All of that tells me that he is a man of some means and one who is quite used to issuing orders and having them obeyed without question. I find the line 'I expect you will make yourself available' most telling."

"A military man, perhaps?" I offered.

"Quite possibly," replied Holmes.

"Given that he declares it to be a matter of 'some urgency – and delicacy,' aren't you even the least bit intrigued?"

"Not at all," replied my friend dismissively. "The 'matter' – whatever it may be – is no doubt considered to be urgent and delicate by Mr. Prescott, but since I know nothing of it, I find it neither. Moreover, I have a number of pressing errands to which I must attend this afternoon."

"Oh? Do tell."

"Yes. I must visit the stationers in order to replenish my supply of paste so that I may add these articles to my indexes," he said brandishing a sheaf of papers that he had culled from the various newspapers which he devoured each morning. "You know how I like to keep things current. In addition, I need to restock my store of tobacco. Pressing business, indeed," he said, tapping the ash from his favorite briar.

"So you are not the least bit curious?"

"I have often wondered, how does one measure curiosity, Watson? Is it in bits or degrees? I have always opted for the latter, although I am fairly certain it can be both."

At that point, I knew there was nothing to be gained in arguing with him when he had already made up his mind. Truth be told, I knew the overbearing tone of the note had nettled my friend. Although my own sense of inquisitiveness was yearning to know more, I decided to accompany Holmes. Secretly I harbored hopes I might be able to steer him back to Baker Street in time to meet with Mr. Prescott.

After we had lunched, Holmes set out on his "pressing errands." It began with a stop at James J. Fox on St. James Street. During the cab ride, Holmes was his usual taciturn self. However, once we arrived at the tobacconist, he became quite animated and began by purchasing enough shag to last him several weeks. Although it is a word I should never have thought to use in describing my old friend, I must say that when it came to replenishing his supply of cigarettes, Holmes positively dithered. Finally, after sampling more than a dozen different types of tobacco and discoursing on the merits of each, he refilled both his cigarette case and mine and purchased several dozen more for the future.

Despite the fact that there was a stationary store on the next block, Holmes insisted we must travel to Harrods, claiming that store alone carried the particular brand of paste that he preferred for his yearbooks. Never having known him to express any particular preference for paste in the past, it finally dawned upon me that just as I was determined to persuade my friend to return to our lodgings, he was equally determined to prolong the afternoon's expedition in order to avoid having to meet with Mr. Prescott.

After Holmes had concluded his performance in Harrods, I glanced at my watch and saw that it was nearing five o'clock. I said to Holmes, "I think you have accomplished your purpose."

"Oh," he remarked, the very picture of innocence, "I wasn't aware I had a 'purpose,' as you put it, aside from procuring tobacco and paste."

"Are you seriously trying to tell me there was no intent on your part to avoid your appointment with Mr. Prescott?"

"Who?" he inquired, and I nearly believed him but for the slight twinkle in his eye.

"Come on, old man. I am certain he has departed by now."

So we hailed a cab and conversed about any number of subjects, from the cases he was working on to the tobacco he had just purchased to his experiments at Montpelier during his absence.

Order appeared to have been restored to the world as we stepped down from the cab in front of our lodgings. However, no sooner had we entered then Mrs. Hudson met us at the foot of the stairs.

"Oh, Mr. Holmes, Dr. Watson, I am so glad you have returned."

"Pray tell, what is troubling you, dear lady?" said Holmes.

"You had a caller arrive a little more than an hour ago. Truth be told, he rang the bell at exactly four o'clock."

Holmes rolled his eyes and then said, "Yes, I was rather expecting him – and hoping to avoid him. I do hope you informed him of my absence and sent him on his way."

"I tried, Mr. Holmes. As God is my witness, I did."

"Tried? Tried? Would you care to elaborate, Mrs. Hudson?"

"I told him that you weren't in, and I had no idea when you'd return."

"And?" inquired Holmes.

"He broke down in tears and begged me to let him wait for you. He said it was a matter of life and death."

"Mrs. Hudson?"

"I'm truly sorry, sir. But he didn't look well, and I didn't have the heart to refuse him. He's waiting in your rooms. I simply couldn't bear to turn him away."

"You have left him alone in our rooms for more than an hour?"

"No, sir. Not at all. I waited with him much of time, but then I had to leave in order to start preparing supper. I do hope you understand, sir."

"We shall discuss this later," said Holmes as he bounded up the stairs. I was right behind him when he threw open the door.

There sleeping in Holmes chair was a young man, perhaps twenty-five or thirty years old. He had a head of thick black hair and appeared to be quite a good-looking fellow. I could easily see how he might have charmed Mrs. Hudson. However, I knew Holmes would not be swayed.

On the table next to the man was a nearly empty decanter of brandy and a single glass.

Turning to me, Holmes seethed, "This is insufferable! The man arranges an appointment to which I have not agreed. Then he shows up uninvited, beguiles our landlady with a sad story and some tears and then drinks himself into a stupor."

With that Holmes strode across the room, shook the fellow by the shoulder and said, "Wake up, you rascal."

So violently had Holmes shaken him that the man toppled forward from the chair and fell on the floor face down.

I bent over him to see if he had been injured in the fall, all the while Holmes kept remonstrating both with himself and our unconscious visitor.

Finally, he paused, looked at me and asked, "Well, just how drunk is he, Watson?"

Having finished a cursory examination, for that was all that was needed, I looked up at Holmes and replied, "He's not drunk. He's dead!"

Also from Richard Ryan

The Vatican Cameos – A Sherlock Holmes Adventure

"An extravagantly imagined and beautifully written Holmes story"
(**Lee Child**, NY Times Bestselling author, Jack Reacher series)

Also from Richard Ryan

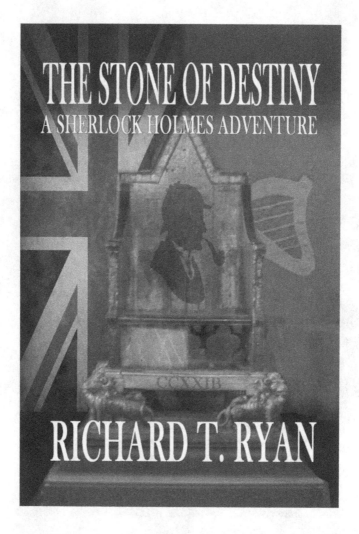

The Stone of Destiny – A Sherlock Holmes Adventure

Also from Richard Ryan

The Druid of Death – A Sherlock Holmes Adventure

"A stunning achievement"
(**Ken Bruen** Author of *The Guards* and creator of Jack Taylor)

Also from Richard Ryan

The Merchant of Menace – A Sherlock Holmes Adventure

Also from MX Publishing

The Detective and The Woman Series

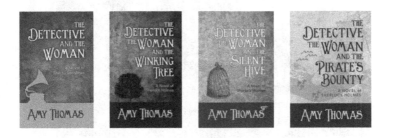

The Detective and The Woman

The Detective, The Woman and The Winking Tree

The Detective, The Woman and The Silent Hive

The Detective, The Woman and The Pirate's Bounty

"I believe the author has hit on the only type of long-term relationship possible for Sherlock Holmes and Irene Adler. The details of the narrative only add force to the romantic defects we expect in both of them and their growth and development are truly marvelous to watch. This is not a love story. Instead, it is a coming-of-age tale starring two of our favorite characters."

Philip K Jones

Also from MX Publishing

The Sherlock Holmes and Enoch Hale Series

The Amateur Executioner
The Poisoned Penman
The Egyptian Curse

"The Amateur Executioner: Enoch Hale Meets Sherlock Holmes," the first collaboration between Dan Andriacco and Kieran McMullen, concerns the possibility of a Fenian attack in London. Hale, a native Bostonian, is a reporter for London's Central News Syndicate - where, in 1920, Horace Harker is still a familiar figure, though far from revered. "The Amateur Executioner" takes us into an ambiguous and murky world where right and wrong aren't always distinguishable. I look forward to reading more about Enoch Hale."
Sherlock Holmes Society of London

Also from MX Publishing

"Phil Growick's, 'The Secret Journal of Dr. Watson', is an adventure which takes place in the latter part of Holmes and Watson's lives. They are entrusted by HM Government (although not officially) and the King no less to undertake a rescue mission to save the Romanovs, Russia's Royal family from a grisly end at the hand of the Bolsheviks. There is a wealth of detail in the story but not so much as would detract us from the enjoyment of the story. Espionage, counter-espionage, the ace of spies himself, double-agents, double-crossers...all these flit across the pages in a realistic and exciting way. All the characters are extremely well-drawn and Mr. Growick, most importantly, does not falter with a very good ear for Holmesian dialogue indeed. Highly recommended. A five-star effort."
The Baker Street Society

Also from MX Publishing

The Conan Doyle Notes (The Hunt For Jack The Ripper)

"Holmesians have long speculated on the fact that the Ripper murders aren't mentioned in the Canon, though the obvious reason is undoubtedly the correct one: Even if Conan Doyle had suspected the killer's identity he'd never have considered mentioning it in the context of a fictional entertainment. Ms. Madsen's novel equates his silence with that of the dog in the night-time, assuming that Conan Doyle did know who the Ripper was but chose not to say – which, of course, implies that good old stand-by, the government cover-up. It seems unlikely to me that the Ripper was anyone famous or distinguished, but fiction is not fact, and "The Conan Doyle Notes" is a gripping tale, with an intelligent, courageous and very likable protagonist in DD McGil."
The Sherlock Holmes Society of London

Also from MX Publishing

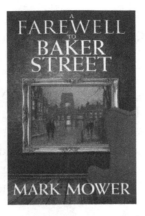

Farewell to Baker Street

Here is a collection of five previously unknown cases from the astonishing career of the consulting detective and his ever-loyal partner. An Affair of the Heart demonstrates the critical interplay between the two men which made their partnership so memorable and endearing. The Curious Matter of the Missing Pearmain is a classic locked-room mystery, while The Case of the Cuneiform Suicide Note sees Dr. Watson using his expert knowledge in helping to solve the mystery surrounding the death of an academic. In A Study in Verse the pair assists the Birmingham City Police in a complicated case of robbery which leads them towards a new and dangerous adversary. And to complete the collection, we have The Trimingham Escapade, the very last case the pair enjoyed together, which neatly showcases the inestimable talents of Sherlock Holmes.

About MX Publishing

MX Publishing is the world's largest specialist Sherlock Holmes publisher, with over four hundred titles and two hundred authors creating the latest in Sherlock Holmes fiction and non-fiction.

Our largest project is The MX Book of New Sherlock Holmes which is the world's largest collection of new Sherlock Holmes Stories – with over two hundred contributors including NY Times bestsellers Lee Child, Nicholas Meyer, Lindsay Faye and Kareem Abdul Jabar. The collection has raised over $60,000 for Stepping Stones School for children with learning disabilities.

Learn more at www.mxpublishing.com

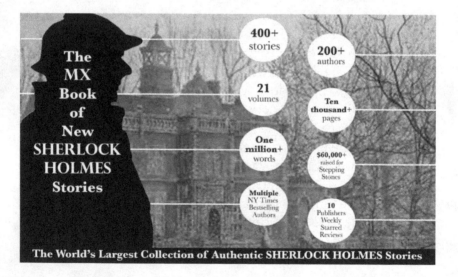

(as of May 2020 – more volumes on the way!)